Montana Secrets

Ann Markworth

Contents

Dedication

I dedicate this book to my IT person, my daughter, Carey Benincasa, who does most of my computer work and my sons, Gordon and Newell Markworth.

Disclaimer

The characters in this book are purely figments of the author's imagination. Any resemblance to persons, living or dead, is coincidental.

About the Author

This is Ann's second novel. Her first one was published one year earlier. Ann was born and raised in Nebraska. She, her husband, and three children moved to the Phoenix area in 1973. She began a 30-year career in the medical field, retiring in 2003. She now resides in the retirement community of Sun Lakes, AZ.

Chapter 1

Buzzy hurried down the hallway of the Grand Ole Opry to Grant's dressing room. Buzzy hurried. That's what Buzzy did. He worried about Grant being late, but he was always on time. Buzzy was taking him to the stage as he did before every show.

Several hours earlier Grant sat in his dressing room and looked in the mirror. He rubbed his face and decided not to put on makeup tonight. It was the local TV stations filming, not the national ones. He went into his small bathroom, washed up and came back out to get ready for the show. He tossed his everyday clothes on the chair and put on his crisp white shirt, buttoned all the way up. He grimaced a little as he buttoned the top button. Tonight, he was wearing his favorite suit, light blue with rhinestones up the side of his pants and decorating his jacket. He grunted as he bent down to put on pants, zipped them up and buttoned the top one. He took a deep breath and went to his dresser and took a bolo tie and belt. He was beginning to sweat. He checked the mirror, brushed his hair and put on his white cowboy hat with the rhinestone band. He started to open the door and realized he hadn't put on his cowboy boots. He grabbed them from the wardrobe and sat down on the chair to struggle into Navy blue boots with rhinestones on the toes. "Whew!" He sighed as he picked up his guitar. Buzzy met him and they went down the hallway together to the stage.

Everyone greeted him as he walked along the hallway, stagehands, other entertainers, his band members. He stood in the wings waiting for the opening band to finish their last song. He noted they were doing an excellent job getting the crowd ready for his entrance. They exited the stage and Grant's band got in position. His theme song started. The crowd jumped to their feet, whooping, hollering and screaming, "Grant! Grant!" He charged onto the stage with his guitar slung over his shoulder and waving his hat wildly. He hollered along with them, and they loved it, He tilted his hat back on at a rakish angle and yelled, "Are you ready to hear the old songs?" They screamed louder and he took a breath. He hit a familiar chord, and the show began.

He enjoyed himself, and since he lived in Nashville, he knew many people in the crowd. He did all the old favorites and tried to introduce a few new ones, but they wanted the old favorites. He did a few encores, then had the boys start the theme song again. He waved to the crowd and walked off the stage.

He walked down the aisle trying to get to his dressing room. The same crowd that wished him well were there to slap him on the back and tell him how great the show was. He smiled at them and took the slaps good-naturedly. He continued to weave through the crowd and entered his dressing room. Buzzy knocked on his door and Grant hollered to come in. "The boys and I are going out to Gilley's for steaks, you want to come along?" "No, I don't think so, but thanks anyway. I just want to get home." "You know we'd like to have you come along, Grant." "I know, but not tonight." "OK catch you in the morning at the studio."

He left his suit on as he planned to take it to the cleaners the next day. He took his other clothes and stuck his head out the door to see if the coast was clear. He hurried to the back entrance and made a dash for his car. Huffing, he got in and drove home. He took a deep breath and relaxed as he entered his driveway and hit the automatic garage door opener. He unlocked his back door and went in. Jake greeted him with a loud meow. Grant reached down and swooped him up and carried him to his bedroom and tossed him on the bed. Grant removed his sweaty suit, then tossed it to the floor. He took a shower and put on shorts and a tee shirt. They returned to the kitchen.

Jake hopped upon the counter. Grant was too tired to push him down. He reached into the pantry for a can of cat food. He gagged as he opened it and put it in Jake's dish. He often wondered if Jake noticed how awful the cat food smelled. He made a peanut butter and jelly sandwich, poured a glass of milk and sat down at the breakfast nook. When they were done eating, they went to the bedroom. Grant sat down on the edge of the bed and turned on the television. He stretched and curled up under the covers. Jake joined him in his usual place on Grant's back and neck. "Damn it!" grumbled Grant as he tossed his covers back and got up. "Mph," said Jake as he jumped down and ran ahead of Grant. They padded to the bathroom and Grant brushed his teeth. They returned to their bed. The television droned as they slept through the night.

Grant Bartlett was a world-famous country western singer/songwriter. He sold millions of albums and singles and wrote many songs for himself and other singers. He wasn't always alone.

Chapter 2

The 6 o'clock alarm buzzed. Bella rolled over to Whit's side of the bed to shut it off. His side was cold, so she knew he'd been up for a while. She rolled back to her side and slipped into her slippers and robe and went to the bathroom. Quickly she finished and hurried down the center stairway and turned left into the kitchen. Whit was sitting at the computer studying the stock market and did not look up. She filled the percolator and walked over to him, bent over, put her arms around him and her face close to his. "Your breath stinks," he said. She dropped her arms and jerked straight up and went to the bathroom off the kitchen and mud room. She took her toothbrush and brushed her teeth vigorously, then rinsed.

She returned to the kitchen, took a slab of bacon from the refrigerator, unhooked a frying pan from the overhead supply of skillets and started frying bacon. Neither of them spoke. Finally, Whit said, "Better call the boys." She moved away from the kitchen and stood at the foot of the stairs. "Breakfast!" "On our way!" Jesse and Jeremy, aged 10 and 12, came tumbling down the steps and dove into their seats at the table. Bella returned to finish cooking and served orange juices and coffee. Still, Bella and Whit hadn't spoken.

"Boys, I'm going to cattle auction this weekend," this was news to her, "and I thought I'd take you along." They whooped for joy. "Settle down! It will be just one night." They made exciting plans. "Whoa up there! Chores are waiting before the school bus comes." They finished breakfast and ran outside.

"I guess I forgot to mention it," he offered. "You probably don't want to go anyway," he hemmed. He got up without another word and left. He was right, she didn't want to go, but it would have been nice if he had asked. She cleared the table and planned her own weekend.

She picked up a flyer that came in yesterday's mail. A well-known country western singer was having a show in Missoula this Saturday night. She remembered she saw an envelope with 2 complimentary tickets for the show. Someone gave them to Whit. He tossed them on the entryway table with no intention of going as he was planning on the cattle show. They were still in the envelope. She opened the envelope and saw the seats were good, in the front-row-center. She perked up. She called her best friend, Tammy, who had never bothered to get married and be tied down. They had been best friends since high school.

"Tammy, what are you doing Saturday night?"

"Why are you calling me this early? You know this is my day off." She was the emergency room nurse at the local hospital. She was married to her job, but in love with the medical director who was married, but she didn't care. She stretched and rolled out of bed. "Ok, I'm up. What have you got in mind? What about Whit? Does he know?" She was not fond of Whit, as Bella and Whit were aware.

"I found tickets to a country-western singer having a show in Missoula tomorrow night. Whit and the boys are going to cattle show somewhere for the weekend, so I thought we could drive down to Missoula and go. I can't stay away from the ranch overnight, but we still can make it back that night. Want to go?" "Who is it?" "Grant Bartlett." "Oh gosh, do you know how famous he is? Of course, I'll go!" "Okay, I'll pick you up early so we can have dinner."

"Who are you talking to?" Whit came in after finishing his chores. "I found the tickets you tossed on the table for a country singer show in Missoula for Saturday night, so thought it would be fun for Tammy and me to go. Won't be overnight." He had forgotten about the tickets. He frowned. She braced for his disapproval. "Just so you get back." "Of course," she promised. "I'm taking Fred and the horses to ride fence. Be back for lunch." She breathed a sigh of relief. She sat down with another cup of coffee to quiet her nerves.

Saturday morning Whit hitched up the cattle trailer just in case he bought more stock. The boys were getting in the way. He scolded them and told them to go get their gear packed. "Have Mom check your gear and get my things ready." They charged into the house and up to their rooms, forgetting what Whit had said. He came in later, wanting to get going. "Where's my stuff," he bellowed. "What stuff?" questioned Bella. "I told the boys to tell you to get my things ready!" he complained. "They never said a thing. I've been working on my stuff to go to Missoula." "Well, get my things, I'm ready to take off! Boys, get down here!" They trooped down the steps with their backpacks. "Bella, take a look at their stuff and get me my things!" Dutifully, she did his bidding. Finally, it was done, and they left. The boys screamed their goodbyes, but Whit only nodded. 'Now it's my turn.' She finished quickly and picked up Tammy. Her mood lightened as she saw her friend. They pulled onto the highway with the radio blaring their favorite songs.

Chapter 3

Bella's parents were high school sweethearts and married right out of high school. Clark was drafted immediately after graduation. They had a quiet wedding just before he left for basic training, Meg got pregnant when Clark came home on leave. He was shipped to Viet Nam after his leave. Meg felt her baby grow without Clark, but she did have the support of her parents. He missed the birth of his daughter, Bella. She was walking when he made it home. Starting out again was hard for both, especially Clark. Soldiers returning were not well received. He got a job at a large supermarket chain stocking shelves. As the years went on, he became store manager. Meg was happy staying home taking care of Bella, then Nancy.

Bella had hazel eyes with lots of brown specks. She had soft dark brown hair that framed her face with curls she never learned to like. When she grew up, she had long curls that hung down to her shoulders. No matter what clothes she wore, they draped over her perfectly. She was kind and sincere, almost to a fault. She quietly did her studies, joined the pep club to yell at football and basketball games, but never dated the players. She never thought about college as she knew her parents couldn't afford it.

Her best friend was Tammy Edwards. Nobody could understand their friendship as Tammy was cute, peppy, a cheerleader and dated all the players she could. Each good point wore off on the other and they were happy with their friendship.

After graduation, Tammy surprised the town, settled down and attended nursing school. She earned a bachelor's degree and became Head of Nursing at the emergency department. Bella took a secretarial course at the local Junior College. Her first and only job was with Hamilton Ranch as secretary and general Girl Friday. Her mother was worried about Bella being around the rough cowboys, but her father thought it would be good for her to get exposed to "how the other half lived." He knew the senior Hamilton due to his large purchases from the supermarket. Clark found him to be pleasant, fair, and perhaps a little gruff.

Tammy was thrilled about Bella's new job. "Geez, Bella, think of all that gorgeous testosterone you will be surrounded by!" Bella was terrified, but was presenting a brave front, especially for her parents, "That fabulous Whit will knock your socks off!" "Oh, for heaven's sake, he won't even look at me!" "Don't count on it, after all you're pretty darn hot yourself!" Tammy tried to bolster her spirits. Bella was a beautiful woman; she just didn't realize it.

Tammy returned to nursing school. Bella drove to the ranch.

Bella turned off the main road onto Hamilton Road and continued to the business buildings and pulled into her allotted covered parking space. Several cowboys exited a building and stopped as they saw Bella getting out of her car. She froze when she saw them coming towards her. They circled around her and examined her and her car. "Well, hi, little lady! You must be the new gal!" One tipped his hat and smiled. Another pounded on the hood of her car, and she jumped. They laughed and continued circling around her and the car. Suddenly, Sam Hamilton yelled from his doorway, "You wranglers get back to work!" They hurried to the horses tied at the hitching post, mounted and galloped off in a cloud of dust. Bella was visibly shaken, still clutching the door handle. "Come on in," he gestured as he held the door open. She felt her legs beginning to move. Her high heels clicked on the white marble tile as she walked with him into his private office. He shut the door.

"The boys meant no harm," he apologized. "Now, do you want a cup of coffee?" He raised his huge coffee cup with the Hamilton logo to his lips. "N-no thanks," she stammered. "Very well then. Let's take a tour and help you get acquainted." Before they could stand up, a tall, handsome cowboy burst into the room. His auburn hair was peeking out from under his grey sweat-stained hat. His dark eyes did not look kindly at Bella, and his thin lips were not smiling. His shirt was chambray blue tucked into Levi's. He wore leather chaps and spurs on his well-worn boots. He was armed with a huge pistol harnessed in a leather holster. The wide leather belt held rows of bullets. He took a seat. He said nothing.

"Good morning, Whit. This is our new office girl, Bella. Bella, this is my son, Whit." Whit said nothing, tipped his hat. His eyes did not meet Bella's. She managed a "Good morning." "Whit will take you to lunch later. I have meetings all day." "I'll be back at noon," said Whit, and abruptly got up and left. 'I'm going to run out of here and quit,' she thought. "Ok," she said with all the muster she could. "Let's take that tour I promised you!" He was irritated at his son's behavior towards his new employee.

They left his tastefully decorated office. The floors were a continuation of the white marble as the reception area, but here Sam Hamilton wanted soft grey on the walls, to show off the huge pictures of his domain. He had pictures of his family displayed in various situations of importance. There was room for them along with floor to ceiling windows that gave views of his expansive land holdings. His desk was knotty pine from his own trees, polished to perfection. His chair was made to match. He had a private bathroom off to one side that had a walk-in shower and closet with extra clothes waiting for unexpected changes. It was tiled from floor to ceiling with mosaic tiles in various shades of blue, his favorite color.

He led her past the reception area and out into the quad. One building housed a well-stocked kitchen, large dining room and restrooms. Permanent staff were available for hungry wranglers, or clients. The dining area could be partitioned for privacy, "You will find that cowboys always come in. You can use this any time you wish." 'I can't see me coming in here, ever,' she mused.

He showed her other buildings that were used for horse equipment and storage. "The corrals and barns are further away, but we won't do that today. I'm sure there will be times when you will go out that way. Let's go back to the reception area and you can get acquainted with your surroundings." They returned to her area. He showed her their computer. He instructed her to let him know what she would need to make her workload comfortable. He planned for Whit to pick her up at noon for lunch. He left for his meetings after giving her a cell phone and showing her where all the important numbers were posted.

She sat down in her beautiful secretary's chair and observed her equally beautiful desk. She ran her hands over the smooth wood and the new computer keys. She explored the drawer contents and found they were already well stocked. She looked at the phone console and hoped she could figure out how to work it. She put her elbows on the desk and cupped her face in her hands and contemplated her life.

Edna Hamilton breezed through the door. Bella started as she did not see her drive up. "Hello!" breathed a well-dressed middle-aged woman who was wearing a turquoise western-cut pant suit with cream-colored cowboy boots with turquoise stitching. Her short snow-white bouffant hair framing her perfectly made -up face.

Turquoise button shaped earrings sparkled with small diamonds as she looked Bella up and down. "I'm Edna Hamilton! I wanted to stop in and introduce myself before I left. I'm off for lunch and bridge." "I'm happy to meet you," stammered Bella. "Make yourself comfortable today and tomorrow we will start training you."

The phone rang. Bella froze, Eda answered, "Hamilton Ranch," she cooed "No he's not here. May I take a message?" She paused and hung up. Bella scrambled to find paper and a pencil. "Never mind this time," Edna said. "I know who it was. I'll tell Sam when he gets home. Here is your first lesson: Never tell the caller where anyone is. Take their name and number and a brief message. If the person is in, give them the message and they will call back if they want. This is probably the most important lesson for you. Now, I'm off to play bridge!" Bella was alone again.

Twelve o'clock came and no Whit. At 12:30 he came storming to the building in a pickup. She was relieved it wasn't a horse. He burst into the room. "Let's go!" He instructed gruffly and turned around and left. She looked around for keys to lock the office and could find none. "I don't have the key!" She hollered out the door. "Geez," he crabbed and rushed back into the office, pulled open a secret door in the wall and retrieved a set of keys. then slammed them down on her desk. "Here," he growled. "I'll lock it this time. You can figure out which one later." She meekly walked out ahead of him as he locked the door and hopped into his side of the truck.

She stood there helplessly trying to open the door. He slid over and yanked it open easily. "Can you get in?" he said rudely. She crawled in and managed to swing it shut. He looked scornfully at her. "Can you get some decent clothes to wear? You don't need high heels and dresses. Wear some jeans and boots. You aren't going to be glued to a desk all the time." She nodded silently. He told her that they would eat lunch at the house.

She held on to the door handle as he barreled down the tree-lined driveway and pulled up by the back entrance. He jumped out of the truck and watched to see if she could get out on her own. He saw that she did. He hurried up the steps and she tagged along. They entered a large wood-paneled mud room. There were benches to sit on while removing wet or muddy boots. Rubber mats were close by to place them. Pegs on the walls held raincoats or heavy jackets. A washstand was for cleaning work-worn hands before entering the kitchen. A large shelf containing fresh towels. A mirror was over the sink for the guys to check their faces and hair. Whit sat on one of the benches to remove his spurs and chaps. He hung his gun belt on one peg and washed up. She watched, fascinated. They entered the kitchen.

It was filled with delicious fragrances of bread baking and pots simmering on the huge gas range. Above was an iron rack stretched across it with various skillets hanging within reach of a cook. On another wall were restaurant size sinks with several faucets and sprayers. The rest of the wall was covered with gleaming countertops and cabinets that reached to the ceiling. On another wall was a double refrigerator-freezer and more gleaming prep areas and cabinets. The room had been constructed with large windows to keep the kitchen bright. The floor had easy -maintenance vinyl. A large wooden table with benches sat in the middle of the room. Bella and Whit sat on stools at a long counter.

A middle-aged plump Spanish woman came over to them. Her smiling face and dark brown eyes looked fondly upon the couple. She was drying her capable hands on her apron that covered up a brightly printed housedress. "Hi, Mr. Whit! What can I get you and this lovely senorita?" she said in her melodious voice. "Maritza, this is our new office girl, Bella," he said with the first cordial voice Bella had heard from him. "We need some lunch, just sandwiches and some iced tea." Maritza smiled at Bella and Bella returned the smile. She quickly brought sandwiches and tea. Whit grabbed his and went upstairs. "He'll be back," Maritza assured her and went back to the tortillas she was making. Bella enjoyed the lunch as she was starving. Whit came back, and they were off to the office. He said more pleasantly, "See you tomorrow. Be sure to lock the door." She explored her new domain and answered a few phone calls. She found the right key, and went home, exhausted.

The first weekend she went shopping. She bought Levi's, which she had never worn in her life. She found comfortable long and short sleeved jersey blouses, a warm jacket and a vest. She had trouble deciding about boots. She was sure she couldn't wear cowboy boots, so she settled on feminine lace-up work boots. She hoped Whit would approve. She thought he never noticed. He did. His parents noticed and complimented her on her choices.

Each day became easier. But ranching was a complicated business and there was much to learn. Mr. and Mrs. Hamilton were excellent and patient teachers. Whit not so much, but they tolerated each other. The Hamilton's had faith in her, and they gave her more responsibilities. She also visited the corrals and barns and tried to touch the horses, but that still hadn't happened. She was learning to accept the cowboys and their rude behaviors and overlook some of the gross things they did.

Tammy came home at Christmas as it was winter break at nursing school. They had not seen each other since Bella started her new job. Bella had the week between Christmas and New Year free. They spent as much time together as possible. Tammy wanted to know all the details about the cowboys, who was cute and who wasn't married and what about Whit? She wasn't interested in the workings of a ranch. Bella filled her in on what she knew, which was very little.

Eddie Walters had worked full-time at the Hamilton ranch for 7 years. Before that, he worked there in the summers during his high school years. His parents wanted him to go to college or the Army, but all he wanted to do was wrangle cattle. Right after graduation he started to work full-time for Sam Hamilton. He loved it. He was tall and thin, but not skinny, Cowboy clothes were made for him. He loved tight jeans, checkered shirts and leather vests. He wore the largest cowboy hat he could find. He had a full drawer of red kerchiefs. He was saving money to buy real leather chaps like Whit Hamilton wore. His thick sandy hair touched the top of his shirt. He was clean shaven, because his whiskers were not thick enough to make a nice beard. He had a sweet smile and kind blue eyes. He was just a nice guy.

He noticed Bella the first day she came to work. He didn't cat-call or make himself obvious to her. He stood back and observed. He found out all he could about her, which wasn't much, but enough to know she was free. He bade his time and waited for her to get used to the ranch. After Christmas he decided to make his move. He bravely stepped into her office when he knew she was alone. She had visited with him several times and he was sure she was not afraid of him. They greeted each other warmly.

"Bella, I would like to take you to the show this Saturday night. What do you say?" he hesitated. She was surprised at the offer and accepted. He was overjoyed and relieved. "Pick you up at seven," he rejoiced and jubilantly ran out the door, mounted his horse, and was ready to take off, when Bella stuck her head out the door. "Do you know where I live?" she yelled. "Of course I do!" He gave a short slap to the horse and galloped away in a cloud of dust. She laughed at his antics. She was looking forward to his company.

Their romance began with that first date. It was simple and easy, revolving into Saturday night dates and visits to each other's homes. Both sets of parents enjoyed their company and were happy with the way the romance was going. During the summer they discussed their goals concerning employment and where their careers were going. There was no advancement in Eddie's. The only possibility was becoming a straw boss. That was tied up with the older bosses who had no plans to retire. Bella had no hope of advancement as she was the only secretary. They said this was not a problem. They hadn't had sex yet. She said she "wasn't ready", but he was. One fall day they made a day trip to Missoula. While walking in the mall they stopped at a couple of jewelry stores to check out rings. Nothing came of it. Tammy was thrilled and wanted all the details about their sex life. She was disappointed. Sam and Edna were enjoying the courtship and hoped they would get married. Their employment would be secure with them if they married. Whit paid no attention.

Chapter 4

Whit had other things on his mind.

Several years ago, he graduated from high school and enrolled in a 4-year course at the University of Montana. His major was business administration. He took all the courses that were required to get his major and did well. What he really wanted to study was soil and land conservation, water management, proper grasslands and animal husbandry. His only goal in life was to manage the ranch with his father, then continue after he retired. He loved the ranch with his whole heart. His grades were excellent. His parents were proud of him, so much that Sam gave him a sports car for college graduation. He knew Whit would take responsibility in caring for it. He had caused them very little stress. Sam's plan was for Whit to take over when it was time.

After graduation, Whit wanted to spend some time with his buddies before settling down. They were glad to accept him back in the fold. He was one of the few guys who had gone to college. They liked to drink beer and cruise the other small towns, "looking for chicks," they said. Whit didn't drink much, so he often found himself the designated driver. During one of their excursions, he saw "her." She was a waitress in a small bar and grille in the next town. Her name was Frankie Knosh. She said she was 19, and Whit believed her. He thought he saw her serving beer. She was tiny with long silky blonde hair. Bangs covered her wide blue eyes. Whit's fingers touched each other when he wrapped his hands around her waist. She loved it when he did that. She could stretch her arms up to his shoulders and rub her ample front on his chest. He loved that too. He would wait for her to finish her shift. They would hurry to his car. She loved the soft leather front seats, but she preferred the back, as did Whit. They would have sex, then she would scurry to the old pickup she drove and go home. She never took Whit to her house.

Once he had to wait for her longer. He ordered a second beer. When she was free, they hurried to his car. They were so busy making love Whit forgot his protection. He was upset with himself. "Oh, honey, don't worry about it! I've done it lots of times and nothing happened," she assured him. Whit was busy feeling angry with himself, so he didn't catch her remark.

One night he came to see her, but she wasn't there. He sat at the bar and ordered a beer from Toots, the bartender. "Where's Frankie?" he asked worried, "Some guy knocked her up and she's not feeling good," Toots informed him dismissively. Whit froze, then left. "Hey, Whit, wait a minute! You forgot to pay!" yelled

Toots. "Oh, yeah," Whit said. He threw down $10.00 and left. Toots picked up the $10.00, tucked it into her pocket, took a large swig of the cold beer, and poured the rest into the sink.

One month later, an older man and a young girl came into the reception area at Hamilton Ranch. The old man was short and skinny and had a scruffy beard. He wore dirty jeans with 2 huge oil stains on the front legs. Dirt was ground into them. His boots had tears between the soles and insteps. The heels were worn to the ground. His flannel shirt was open at the neck and revealed a grimy white tee shirt with brown nicotine stains around the collar. Stringy grey hairs stuck out from under his decrepit baseball cap. The small girl standing beside him wore blue jeans and a flannel shirt, both much too big. Her tennis shoes were more grey than white. Her long flaxen hair was hanging out from a ski cap. She was on the verge of tears.

"I wanna talk to Sam Hamilton," he stated.

"I'm sorry," began Bella, "He's not here at the moment." Sam came blustering through the door.

"What have we here?" he said sternly.

"I wanna see you," the man answered.

"Come into my office. What do you want?" he instructed. The man jerked the girl along with him.

"My name is Frank Knosh, that's with a K. Your son got my Frankie pregnant, and I want $100,000 to keep my mouth shut."

"What?"

"You heard me," Frank said with more gusto. "I want $100,00 to keep quiet,"

Sam stared at him. "I'll have to talk to my son. Leave your name and phone number and I will get back with you." Sam dismissed him.

Frank was hoping Sam would give him the money right then, but he did as Sam asked. He left the info with Bella. She watched them leave. They got into an old pickup. A huge yellow dog was sleeping in the pickup bed. He lifted his head to see what was going on, then went back to sleep.

Sam was livid. He walked to his private liquor cabinet hidden in the wall and pulled out a bottle of bourbon. He carried it to his desk, got a small glass and poured a stiff drink. He downed it with one swallow. It burned his throat and he gagged slightly. He put the bottle back and left his office. "Lock up and go home," he told Bella and left.

He drove home and entered the kitchen. "Edna!" He bellowed. "In our office!" She answered. He burst into the room. "Where is Whit?" He demanded. "He's not here yet. What is it?" She was alarmed. Whit walked into the room. "What's wrong?" He, too, was alarmed. Sam turned around and glared at his son. "Did you get some 17-year-old girl named Frankie pregnant? He and his daughter came to the office demanding $100,000 to keep their mouths shut, as he put it. Well?" Sam waited.

"No, uh, I don't know. How do they know it was me?" He did not know she was only 17. This was more startling news. He was stalling, trying to gain his composure. "She's had other guys, she told me so." But he knew she hadn't been with anyone else since they had been together these last months.

"Sounds like you are confessing, so, is it true? Answer me!"

"Oh, God, Dad, I guess it is true!" His heart was breaking for his parents. They were crushed.

"I don't see any sense doing any testing. This would just be more chance for this to get out. I will call Charley Hollingsworth to work on a document of some kind and then we will meet with this Frank. The money doesn't bother me as much as the girl being pregnant. Just so they don't want you to marry her."

He called Charles Hollingsworth, their attorney they had for many years. They worked out a plan, then met with him in Missoula a few days later. The first problem to solve was what was going to happen to Frankie. They hoped she would settle on an abortion. Charley met with the Knosh's personally. He was surprised how easily they consented to the abortion if Sam would pay for it. After that, he would give them the $100,00. Arrangements were made for Frankie to have the abortion in another state. Edna went with her. They had a private Jet fly them to another state. The 17-year-old

Frankie was thrilled to ride in the jet, no concern over what she was doing. Fake names were used all around and cash flowed abundantly. Charley brought the documents and $100,000 in cash to the Hamilton mansion. Sam, Edna, Whit and Charley met with the Knosh's. They signed the documents, then were handed the cash. They disappeared and Whit thought it was over.

But it wasn't. A few weeks later Sam informed Whit they were going back to meet with Charley again, no reason given. They drove to Missoula to Charley's office. Sam and Edna were quiet. Charley had a long face when they entered his office. "Let's go into the conference room for more privacy," Charley stated. He told his secretary they were not to be disturbed. He shut the door.

"Whit," Charley began, "your parents have been conferring with me since the thing with the girl happened. We have been discussing changes that need to be made. They did not do this lightly. Many hours were devoted to discussions, and, I am sure, a few tears were shed. "

Whit was beginning to sweat. He noticed his parents were different. He looked at the sad expressions on their faces.

"Whit, there must be consequences for what you did. Your parents could not let that go without some changes. They have a document that has been established that will need your signature when this conference is finished. Due to the severity of your actions, this is the proposal written up for you:

You are to court, then marry Bella Archer, within six months of the day you sign this document, which they hope will be today. You will be faithful to her from the first day on. You will provide for her in every way that a supportive and loving husband does. If you have children, they are to be provided for in the same way. You will always respect your family. If you agree to these terms, the ranch and all its holdings will be yours as promised before. If you feel you do not wish to do this, we insist you leave immediately. You will be considered disowned. Your father will give you one million dollars to begin a new life. You will never set foot on Hamilton soil again. Do you accept this proposal?"

Whit thought he was going to vomit. He was sweating profusely. His shoulders were shaking. He looked at his parents and he saw they meant it, even though his mother had tears in her eyes and his father could not look at him. He found his voice.

"But I'm not in love with Bella! I don't want to marry her or have children or live up to any of this stuff you have offered me!"

"Then you just want the million dollars and leave?"

Whit asked to be excused and ran out the door. He frantically looked for the restroom. He made it to the toilet and vomited. When he was finished, he washed his face and went back into the conference room.

"I will marry Bella in 6 months," he said, and fainted. When he came to, he signed the documents. They went back to the ranch.

Monday morning Whit waited for Bella to come in. She was startled when she saw him sitting there. "What are you doing here?" she asked him. "Oh, not much, just having a cup of coffee. Do you want one?" "What? A cup of coffee?" "Yes. Why don't I go and get you a cup," he offered. 'That is strange,' she thought. He went on before she could answer, "Cream and sugar, or black?" "Black," she said, still wondering what was going on. He left and was back in no time. "Thank you," she said. He sat there for a few minutes drinking coffee with her. "Back to the salt mines," he grinned, and left. She sat drinking her coffee, still puzzled.

This went on for a few weeks until she became used to him coming in. Eddie noticed it too and asked her about it. She explained she didn't know. Eddie didn't like it, but he couldn't do anything about it since technically Whit was his boss. All he could do was keep an eye on the situation.

One morning he came in and told her he was going to another ranch to check out some horses they were thinking about purchasing. He did not need her to go, but he told her to bring along her notebook to keep track of the horses. He had the forms in his briefcase but didn't tell her. She dutifully put away her work, grabbed her notebook, and got in the pickup. They drove to the next ranch and kept up a good stream of conversation. The possible horses were herded into the corral. She expertly took notes as he dictated to her. The cowboy herding the horses gave Whit a bad time about his "secretary." Going home, they again continued their pleasant conversation. He gallantly retrieved her notes and put them in with his other notes in his briefcase. He thanked her for her time and left. He showed both sets of notes to Sam. He was impressed with what she wrote, even though it was under false pretentions.

He continued with his coffee visits two or three times a week and invited her on excursions. She enjoyed and expected these new events in her life, but Eddie didn't. She wasn't sure how to handle these situations, so she ignored them.

This went on for five months and Whit had to do something. Six months were looming. Christmas and New Years came and went, and the earth was beginning to bloom. One warm Montana spring day Whit took Bella on a tour of the ranch she hadn't seen. There was a small brook that meandered through the pastures that were fed by runoff from the mountains. A sandy beach was surrounded by trees. Wildflowers were blossoming close by. He wanted to take her there. He didn't tell her exactly where they were going. She was enjoying this new adventure and the exquisite views. She had no objection when he stopped the pickup by the small beach. She ran to the stream and ran the clear water through her fingers. They sat on the sandy beach for a while. He rubbed the back of her neck. It felt so good. She could feel the sun on her face. Her eyes closed slightly. He reached down and brushed her lips gently. He kissed her again and she returned his kisses. He removed her clothes, even her boots and slowly made love to her. She didn't know what to do, so she clung to him. Later he held her close until her eyes flew open. He handed her clothes to her and stepped away while she dressed. She was lacing her boots when he came back. He helped her to the truck. He held her close to him until they got to her car. He reached for her purse, took her keys and unlocked the car for her. "Can you drive?" He asked her kindly. She nodded. He watched her drive away, then headed up to the house. He found his parents watching television in the family room. "It's done. You can start planning the wedding for the last Sunday of the month," he said. He left. His parents looked at each other and smiled.

Bella walked into the kitchen where her mother was standing at the sink. Meg looked into Bella's knowing eyes and saw the swollen and bruised lips. The question stood between them. "Yes," said Bella and went to her room. Meg sat down and buried her face in her hands. She decided not to tell Clark yet.

Sunday, he went to her house. She was expecting him. They sat on the couch. He put his arm around her, and she put her hand on his thigh. Her parents beamed and Nancy giggled. They were planning the wedding. It would be the last Sunday of the month. They would get married in her church. The reception would be held in the country club, as Sam and Edna were members. Nancy would be her maid of honor and Tammy a bridesmaid. She would rather have Tammy, but it was only fitting that Nancy should be the maid of honor. Tammy agreed. Whit would have his two best friends for his attendants. All the important things were decided, now the fun things could begin!

Bella, Meg, Nancy and Tammy chose what needed appointments first. The country club would serve a light dinner as the wedding would be at 3 p.m. A wine and beer open bar would be provided. The country club chef would bake a 3-tiered wedding cake because Sam and Edna would have a much larger guest list than Meg and Clark. Spring flowers would be ordered from the local florist. Bouquets and corsages would also be fresh flowers. A photographer from Missoula would be taking all the pictures. Meg thought she should check on Nadine, the organist. She was available, so Bella chose the music she wanted. The pastor was contacted right away. "I think I can get a little nap after my sermon and before the wedding!" He teased.

They went over the list again and again and agreed appointments had been set. They were ready to choose the wardrobes!

The guys were the easiest. Whit had a grey western cut dress suit with narrow pin stripes in the jacket. He owned good black dress boots. He purchased a new white western dress shirt. His father gave him his silver cuff links and his mother gave him a new silver bolo tie. Bella approved of his outfit. "It wouldn't matter to me what you wore, Whit, you are handsome in jeans!" she gushed, and he turned away. The guys rented black wester cut suits and purchased new black boots they could always wear later. Sam, of course, had a dress western suit. Clark broke the theme by wearing a regular dress suit, which was okay by all.

Trying to please two girls wasn't as easy. Nancy wanted a chiffon flowing long skirt with long sleeves and high neckline. Tammy wanted a short skirt, plunging neckline and no sleeves. Bella said we must compromise! After much haggling, they chose long slim skirts with a slash up the back with Nancy's much less that Tammy's, scoop necklines and cap sleeves. Blue and pink spring colors were chosen for the dresses. Their slippers were dyed to match. Bella gave them necklaces with one pearl and small diamonds around it on silver chains as gifts.

Bella, Meg and Nancy went to the large bridal shoppe in Missoula. The first one she tried on was perfect, but Meg thought she should try on a few more. She was exhausted after trying half a dozen. They came back to the first one and Meg was sorry she asked Bella to try on the others. The skirt was made of silk and had crinoline underneath. The bodice had a mock turtleneck and long fitted sleeves that came to points over her wrists. The pillbox veil's train fell past her waist. A small veil could be placed over her face for the first part of the ceremony. No alteration was needed, but the shoppe kept it to press and would deliver it the day before the wedding.

The night before the wedding, Sam and Edna hosted the wedding rehearsal dinner at the supper club in town. It was elegant and quiet and had a separate dining room for events like this. Everyone could choose their own meal and drinks. The staff worked diligently preparing the dinner as Sam was a frequent user of their facilities.

The group met at the church for the rehearsal. There were a few glitches. The groomsmen kept snickering and pushing Whit until Whit finally had enough. Nancy and Tammy were continually flirting with the groomsmen until Pastor Henry scolded them. Bella took everything seriously and Whit wished it was over. The parents sat in the front pew trying not to laugh so they wouldn't get in trouble too. The harried pastor dismissed them, and they piled into cars with laughter following them to the restaurant. Pastor Henry was the first one at the bar for a glass of beer. Good times continued for some time.

The day of the wedding was perfect. Edna hosted an early brunch. The house was filled with chaos. At one o'clock, everyone but Bella began to get ready. The guys went upstairs to Whit's suite. While up there, Greg had a bottle he was keeping for sharing when they were alone. The guys took good swallows, but Whit did not. They didn't know, but this was not a joyous occasion for him. Downstairs, the girls donned their gowns and left for the church. Meg, Nancy and Tammy helped load the car with Bella and her gown, still in the garment bag. They went into the dressing room. Bella dressed with their help. Meg's heart was filled with hope and love. Tammy and Nancy said she was the most beautiful bride ever.

Sam, Edna and Clark welcomed the guests in the narthex. Pastor Henry came to retrieve the male party. Meg came to join them. Tom and Greg took each mother's arm with Sam tagging along to their front row seats. Just then Bella appeared. Clark thought he would cry. She looked so beautiful that she took his breath away. He walked to her and said, "Are you ready, Bella?" "Yes, daddy, I am," she whispered. Tammy and Nancy walked to their positions. The Wedding March began, and everyone stood up. Bella and Clark walked down the aisle. Whit made himself look at her. They got to the chancel and Clark stepped back and sat with Meg. Whit reached for her and guided her to the altar. 'My God', he thought. 'She is beautiful! I never noticed. She deserves better than me.'

The country club reception was fabulous. The first dances went off without a hitch. Greg gave a decent toast. The cake was cut, and the bouquet and corsages were thrown. The bride and groom stepped away when no one was looking. They drove to the mansion and changed clothes. Bella wore creme colored slacks and a soft green sweater. Whit slipped on jeans. They took their suitcases and went to the sports car. Sure enough, the guys found it and tied tin cans to the bumper. Whit worked them loose. They drove to Cor'de Alane, Idaho, and checked into the hotel by the lake.

Eddie cried that day and planned on quitting the next. Sam said, "Hold on now! Ralph is retiring, and I plan to replace him with you. You are now a straw boss!" Eddie got ahold of himself.

Chapter 5

Grant was born in Louisville, Kentucky. His mother was a schoolteacher and his father worked for the post office. Louise quit teaching until Grant was 8. When he was six, Louise enrolled him with Miss Suzanne, the school's music director who gave lessons in her home. Grant hated it, but he did learn to read music. He would never be a piano virtuoso. When he was ten, he saw 'The Singing Cowboy,' Gene Autrey. He pestered his father, rather than his mother, for a guitar. He figured he would have better luck with him. He did. John Bartlet and Grant went to the second-hand music store and purchased a guitar. The new teacher became a guitar teacher and Miss Suzanne retired. Grant did well with the young teacher, whose main job was playing in a local country western band. He stayed with the guitar and teacher through high school. He started writing songs when he was 15. He played them in school, church, or any group that would listen. By the time he was a senior, he was making money with gigs, playing both his songs and covering popular ones. After graduation he informed his folks that he was going to Nashville and try his luck with recording studios and gigs. He had no intention of going to college. They said no but he went anyway.

Grant knew Peggy in high school. He became acquainted with her their senior year. She loved his music and tried to go to all his gigs. He took her with him when she was free. She honestly loved his work, but the more time they spent together, she realized she was falling in love with him. He felt the same. They were surprised about this turn of events. She knew he was going to Nashville after graduation, and she had four years of college ahead of her. So, he left for Nashville, and she started her freshman year at college. Both did well, Grant making money and she was getting 'smarter.' They came home for Thanksgiving and were inseparable. Christmas came and they knew they were going to get married. Their parents said no. They went to Knoxville, found a Justice of the Peace to marry them once they proved they were old enough. Her parents were shocked and disappointed, but Grant's folks seemed to take it well. Peggy packed her things, and they left New Year's Day for Nashville. They stayed in a motel until they could find an apartment. He had recordings and gigs, and she had fun fixing up the very small apartment. She found she missed school, but tried to make the best of it and found a job in a drug store pharmacy department.

Grant's career was booming. He began to get gigs in other towns. It wasn't long before he got shows in other states. He had put together his own band. He played rhythm guitar, so he hired a lead guitarist. A bass player and drummer complete the band. They named it 'The Kentuckians.' A 'tongue in cheek' name since they were in Tennessee, but 'Tennesseans' sounded weird. An agent and bookkeeper were needed. These things kept Grant on the go and absent. Peggy could not go with him anymore, nor was she able to do the business end. After a few years, she got jealous of his success and was worried he was cheating on her. He was not. He could have, but he still was in love with her. She was the one weakening. After five years of marriage, she had divorce papers drawn up while he was in Texas. He was devastated. "Are you sure we can't work this out? I love you, Peggy!" "Nope. I'm done. Going home and go back to school, if my folks will take me." In a way he was glad they never invested in a house. He continued to stay in the little apartment filled with memories. He wrote lots of top hits while staring at those walls, sad songs that made the girls cry. This made him more popular than ever. He enjoyed the company of some of these ladies. He soon discovered this was not as much fun as he thought. There were women he was seeing whose boyfriends and husbands did not like that arrangement. After a few years, he cleaned up that part of his life. It was healthier before he got shot.

He still didn't need a house, but after several years of being teased by his bandmates, he started shopping for a house in Brentwood. He was still paying rent for this little hole in the wall, making his landlord a happy guy taking his rent and never fixing anything. Grant didn't think to ask him for paint or new flooring. Finding just the right house took a lot longer than he thought it would. He never was there to look. He went through several real estate agents before he finally found one that had the patience to wait for him. He returned from a tour and found a phone message saying she had found the perfect house for him. 'Yah, right!' he thought. But he was excited as she knew what he wanted. Polly Wilson picked him up the next day. They pulled into the driveway of this exquisite house set up on a small rise. It was sprawling red brick with a huge white trimmed picture window close to the entryway. The entryway was a masterpiece. Huge wooden double doors were encased in white trim. High up on the doors were arched glass windows. Chandeliers from the foyer glowed through the glass. Old shade trees graced the front yard. Bushes were placed close to the house but did not obstruct any white trimmed windows. He stood there entranced. "Shall we go in?" she asked soothingly.

She went ahead of him, unlocked the door and stepped aside. He quietly entered the foyer, stepping on dark polished tile. The house was empty, but the chandeliers spread their soft light into corners. They turned to the right and entered the living room. He looked out the picture window and liked what he saw. Looking back into the room, he stared at the red brick fireplace that took up half the wall. The hearth and mantle were covered in the same dark tile as the foyer. The floor had rich beige carpet that continued into the dining room. They entered the kitchen. All new stainless-steel appliances had been installed. Ample dark oak cupboards and cabinets completed the room. They went through the rest of the house and premises. The back yard had a pool with a cabana. There was an attached three car garage. He loved it all.

The deal was completed as quickly as real estate sales happened, and he was moved in about a month. He figured he had the rest of his life to furnish and decorate it. He was a happy man.

Grant never thought he was 'handsome,' but he was. He wasn't six feet tall, but he wasn't short, either. He was stocky with broad shoulders and strong arms. He had a firm handshake. His legs were sturdy from all the years of standing on the stage. His hair was thick and golden, but his eyelashes and brows were soft brown hiding his deep blue eyes. A nice nose and firm jaw framed a thin mouth until he smiled. Then his face would become animated.

Chelsea Dupre thought he was handsome. She was a journalist/writer for a Canadian Entertainment Magazine. Her editor assigned her to do a story on him. They set up an appointment for her to interview him at his studio between tours. She jumped at the chance. The day of her interview, she took time to get ready in her hotel room. She chose a navy-blue suit with a short skirt that came six inches above her bare knees. Her jacket was tight cut, long sleeved, and one button to close it. She wore no bra. Blue Jimmy Chu high heeled pumps graced her slim ankles and smooth-shaved legs. Her dark hair flowed over her shoulders and rested on the front of her jacket. Her make-up was perfect with bright red lipstick. "There! I should be able to get all the juicy information from him!" She was known to get information from important people who didn't mean to divulge their secrets. He was sitting at the piano when she arrived.

"Come in!" he said graciously. She swiveled her hips into the room and pulled a chair up close to face him. She crossed her legs and took out her small recorder.

"I've so wanted to meet you!" She gushed. "I have tons of questions I plan to ask you!'

"Don't take too long. I have people coming in soon." He turned back to the piano. She pulled her chair closer to him.

"What are you working on?" she asked.

"New songs."

"Can't you tell me what they are?" She flipped her hair coquettishly.

"Nope"

She continued with more mundane questions and was getting nowhere with him. She tried a different approach. He flipped through some music sheets. She crossed and recrossed her legs.

"Have you been seeing anyone new that my readers would be interested in hearing about?" she wheedled.

He slammed the sheet music down on top of the piano and stood up. "That topic is not up for discussion. The interview is over. I would like to suggest the next interview with a man that you wear something more dignified than short skirts and Jimmy Chu shoes."

For once she was speechless. No man had ever turned her down like Grant Bartlett did. She stood up, pulled at her skirt and left. He sat back down at the piano and snickered. When the new issue came out, he noticed the article was short.

There would be times when new band members were needed. Sometimes family issues would interfere, or one might think he could get a better deal. This happened several years after the start of the group. Art, the bass player, had to leave. He didn't want to, but family duty called. "Can you at least finish this tour?" Grant pleaded. "Okay, but that's it," Art promised. Grant got the word out while on tour and in Nashville. They got back and still no takers. One evening he was getting ready to leave the studio. He shut off the lights and opened the door. He was startled to see a girl, at least he thought it was a girl. She was thin and had on tight jeans and a hoodie. "What are you doing here?" he challenged. "Are you looking for a bass player?" "Yes, but," he began. She reached down and picked up her bass guitar and pushed her way into the studio. "You play something," she instructed. She began playing. Grant decided to humor her and sat at the piano and started playing one of his songs. She immediately picked up the bass part. They continued playing for half an hour. "Well, I guess you are hired," he offered and wondered if he made a mistake. "Thanks," she said and went to the door.

"Uh, is that your van?" he asked. "Yep. Also, my home," she volunteered as she opened the door. "You don't have a home?" "No not right now." "You can't sleep in that! It's cold!" "You got a better idea?" "Tell you what, you can come home with me and park the van in my back yard. For now, you can sleep in a spare bedroom," he couldn't believe he was hearing what he was saying. "Ok," she chirped. She followed him home and parked where he pointed.

She took a plastic bag from the van and followed him. He hoped she didn't have a gun. He still wondered if he made a mistake. He took her to his spare bedroom. She plopped her things on the bed and turned around to look at him. He relaxed somewhat. "Where's the bathroom?" She asked and took it upon herself to look for it. She went in and shut the door. "Uh, if you need anything, let me know," he offered. No reply.

The next morning, she was in the kitchen banging pots and pans. "Where's the coffee?" she greeted him. "Right there in front of you," he snapped back. "Ok," she ignored him and made coffee. He shut his mouth and made breakfast. They ate in silence.

'I really would like to know your name," he asked over coffee. "My name is Ricky Tricone," she offered. "Uh, Ricky?" "Yes. My mother liked Ricky Ticky Tavy," she explained. "What?" "It's a kid's book." "Whatever," he replied, and shook his head. They cleaned the kitchen and left for the studio.

The band was warming up when they got there. They stopped dead when Grant and Ricky walked in. "Boys, this is our new bass player, for a while, anyway." No response. "Wait till you hear her!" he gushed. Stares. "Ok, come on, let's go!" Grudgingly they took their places and barely made room for her. Grant growled at them. Suddenly there was room.

After half an hour, they were still speechless, this time with amazement. They understood why Grant brought her in to play with them. But they were not warming up to her. Grant let that go for now. They had local gigs for the next few months and would be traveling by bus. Grant gave her his room and bunked with the boys. They were furious with this arrangement but were angrier when they found out she was living with Grant. He finally had to talk to them. "You know we are doing better than ever; you can't deny that. Records are selling, even with her name on the label. We are making money hand over fist." "Are you sleeping with her too?" Rick couldn't resist. Grant's hands turned into fists and his face grew ugly. Rick stood up expecting a punch. Grant released his fists. "No. I will answer that, even though it's none of your business. Simmer down." That was all he could muster before something serious happened. The guys had their own meeting after Grant left. They talked about leaving the band, but Grant was right, the money was rolling in and they were getting their share, and Ricky was good.

Things were going well at home. Grant and Ricky had settled into a nice routine. She did help around the house and even cooked. Some of it went into the disposal, but most of it was edible. She tried to sneak a cigarette into the house a few times. But Grant could always smell it. She didn't like feeling his wrath, so she quit. One night several months later, Grant opened his bedroom door just as Ricky was coming out of her bathroom in a robe. They stopped and stared at each other. It seemed like forever until Grant led her into his bedroom. She slept with him off and on. Gradually she brought her clothes into his bedroom drawers and closets and her toiletries into his bathroom. This quiet arrangement went on for five years. They never invited anyone over, so they kept their secret safe. Grant was so happy he was able to write some terrific country-western love songs that sold as albums. They topped the country-western charts for weeks.

One day Ricky told Grant she wanted to spruce up her van. She said she loved that van and wanted to keep it in good running condition. He gave her his credit card. She used it to fill the gas tank, along with the van repairs. Two days later, Grant had an appointment with his accountant. After he left, she loaded her things in the van, then went into the kitchen and poured a fresh cup of coffee. She got a saucer from the cupboard and lit a cigarette, using the saucer as an ashtray. She went into his office and took a piece of his personal stationery. She took it back to the kitchen and wrote: "I'm leaving you, Grant. It's been fun but I'm done." She ground out the cigarette in the saucer and put the note under it. She left his credit card. She had no intention of leaving a trace. She left the door unlocked, unlocked the gate and drove away without shutting the gate. She stopped at her bank and drew out all her money but did not close the account. She pulled onto the interstate and was gone.

The first thing Grant noticed when he drove into the driveway was the gate was wide open. Startled, he continued to drive into his back yard. He saw the back door was open too. Panicked, he ran into the kitchen yelling "Ricky!" No answer. He ran through the house calling her name. He ran into his bedroom and saw the drawers and closet were open. Glancing into the bathroom he saw the same situation. Everything of hers was gone. He was beginning to sweat. He ran back to the kitchen where he saw the mess on the table. He grabbed her note and read it. Furious, he picked up the dirty saucer and started to throw it away, then shook his head and ran outside to the trash barrel and threw away the butt. He saw the credit card when he came back in. He stopped to catch his breath and put the card back into his wallet. He put the dirty dishes in the sink and wadded up the note and tossed it in the garbage can under the sink. Now he was breathless, along with the sweating. He felt the coffee pot and found it still warm, so he sat down with it and drank what was left.

"Ugh," he said as he swiped his mouth with his sleeve. "That ungrateful bitch," he fumed.

He rested there until he calmed down. He went to his liquor cabinet and pulled out a bottle of bourbon and a glass. He sat down in his recliner and poured a drink. He sipped his drink until he noticed it was dark and he was hungry. He ordered a pizza and tipped the pizza boy an exorbitant amount. "Gee, thanks, Mr. Bartlett!" he exclaimed and couldn't wait to tell his co-workers about his huge tip. Grant turned on the television, poured a large glass of bourbon, ate the whole pizza, drank the glass of bourbon, and passed out in the recliner.

The phone rang at 8 a.m. the next morning. He reared up from his chair to answer it. "Hey, Grant, are you coming in today?" Rick inquired. "Uh, No. I'm not. Will see you in the morning," he managed to explain. He abruptly hung up and wobbled to the bathroom. He was sure he had never been that sick in his life, and probably never was. Later he crawled into his bed and slept till the next morning.

He felt better the next day. He was ashamed of himself for tying one on like that, but he figured he paid for his mistake. He showered and picked up coffee and a light breakfast on his way to the studio. He was dreading facing the boys.

"I've got news for you," he said after taking ribbing from the guys. "Ricky is gone. She packed up yesterday after getting her van in shape, thanks to my credit card. She took her stuff and left the door and gate wide open. She left me a note and a cigarette butt!" The guys tried not to cheer; they would do that later. Grant had to go over the story again. Then he got down to business.

"There are three things we must do. The first, of course, is to find another bass player. Second, I am going to hire a road manager to keep track of us and our equipment and set up gigs and tours. I will need someone with band experience and can tour with us. The third thing is really for me. I must find a housekeeper to keep me in shape!" They laughed at the last one. "That's all for today. Go out and hustle and find a bass player that is at least half as good as Ricky was." Grant left them to give them time to discuss the situation. They felt bad for the bender Grant went on because he did not do those things. They were getting so popular and famous; they did need a road manager. Fans often slowed them down and found it was hard to get to the bus or airport. They did make a few snide remarks about his need to find a "housekeeper" like Ricky. Grant had not fooled them.

He went home to compose the ads. First, he posted he wanted an experienced bass player, preferably male. He used the business phone number, rather than his personal number. He was sure his need for a base player spread quickly. Next, an experienced country-western band manager who would be able to tour with the band, again using his business phone. Now came the hard one, where to start. He had gotten used to Ricky's help around the house, although it was not always good, but often pleasant. He was not looking for the other benefits she provided. He scribbled on his pad:

"Wanted, housekeeper." He scratched his head looking for the right words. "Prefer cleaning and some cooking. Able to stay if entertainer was on tour, prefer mature lady." Now he decided to use his personal unlisted phone number. He didn't want a high school girl looking for a way to "entertain" him. He sighed and shook his head, feeling this was a stupid ad. He called a few newspapers and entertainment magazines and placed the ads.

Rick took care of the bass player that night. He called Grant.

"You're not going to believe this! We stopped at Gilley's for a beer. Guess who joined us? Huey Messersmith!"

"What?"

"Yes! He quit today! He said he just couldn't stand Barney falling off the stage drunk. They had to close the show last night. The audience threw beer cans at them. They told Barney if he didn't go to rehab, they were finished. Frankly, he had it and is ready to move on. I told him we're looking for a bass player and he was thrilled. I told him to come in tomorrow!"

"Well, I'll be damned! I wouldn't have needed to place the ad today!"

Huey was talking about one of Grant's biggest competitors in Nashville. The lead singer wrote many of his own songs and for others. His wife left him a few months ago. She was tired of his infidelity and heavy drinking. Everyone in the music field knew of his plight and was not surprised about what happened last night. Hopefully, he would take his band members' advice.

Grant was anxious to get to the studio to interview Huey. As far as his musical ability, there was nothing to question. All they had to do was agree on wages and benefits. Huey fit in with the band members and they were looking forward to ironing out everything and beginning touring.

Calls began coming in for the road manager. Grant decided to stay home the next day to filter them. Many of them were ridiculous, but he could expect that, considering the business he was in. He wished he had asked for a college degree. A few were young boys looking for a way to get into the music field. He realized his next mistake was he didn't ask for a male. Groupies were sure they could handle everything the guys 'needed.' He finally found two guys he was interested in. The first one did have a bachelor's degree in business. The young man arrived in a new Lexus. Grant watched him walk up to his door and ring the bell. He was dressed in a Brookes Brothers suit. Grant thought of hiding, but he bravely let him in. Fergus Weiner III handed a limp hand to Grant to ingulf into his. Fergus quickly drew his white manicured hand back.

"Come into the kit-uh, my office," offered Grant. He thought Fergus would not be comfortable in a kitchen.

"Ok," said Fergus. He wanted to wipe the chair before he sat down.

"I thought since you had a degree in business, you might be able to keep track of everything in order," he opened.

"Yes, sir," Fergus said, "Every penny will be accounted for." He looked defiantly at Grant.

"No, not the money. I mean the band equipment and their wardrobes after a show."

"You mean those dirty instruments and sweaty clothes?" he gasped.

"Yes, all of that," stated Grant.

Neither was sure which one tried the hardest to end the interview. Fergus ran to his Lexus and sped away.

His next interview was scheduled for 2 p.m. the next day. That morning Grant made a long list of questions on his legal pad. He figured he would be ready for anything this new guy could come up with. At exactly 2 p.m., Hiram 'Buzzy' Williams rang the doorbell. Grant opened the door, looked him over, and decided he could interview him in the kitchen.

"Come in, uh, Hiram," Grant began, a little uncomfortable.

Buzzy laughed and said, "Call me Buzzy. My dad named me that when I was a toddler, because he said I buzzed around the house on my tricycle. Hiram is an old family name, and I am the first boy, so I got stuck with it. I'm very happy to meet you in person, Mr. Bartlett. I have seen you many times in concert."

"Thanks! You have some idea what I am looking for, I imagine. I see you were with Dusty and his bluegrass band for several years. I've been on stage with him a few times. Suppose that was the time you saw me. I will need probably about the same things as Dusty needed; making sure instruments and costumes are loaded, and generally keeping an eye on what's going on. It's amazing how important it is for your ability to keep up in situations. I should have looked for a road manager a lot sooner. Why are you leaving him?"

"I was with him over 15 years. I've been married for 12 years and have 4 kids. Mary Lou wants to come home to Franklin to raise the kids. Her family is there, and she gets lonely when I'm on the road. Now, I want you to understand, she is a remarkable woman and is willing to spend weeks without me when I'm on tour with the band. We are very happy together and we don't mess around, which is rare, but some of us are faithful," he explained.

"Yes, that is something I had in mind to ask you Believe it or not, my boys are OK, too."

"I know. I did some checking up because I didn't want to get involved with possible bar fights or shootings!" They chuckled.

Buzzy had gone back several years with his quest. He found out Grant had had his fun when he first started but it was over now.

"I want to take you to the studio tomorrow and meet the boys. I think if everything goes well, we can get a contract signed and begin to plan tours with the business end. I want to tour in the Northwest before it gets cold and end up in Vegas for 3 nights."

Buzzy left the interview with a happy mind and was anxious to tell Mary Lou she could start packing for the move back to Franklin.

Buzzy was 6 feet 4 inches with no fat on his ribs. He had brown curly hair and horn-rimmed thick glasses. His brown eyes peered through the lenses with concern, but he could stare into a troublemaker's eyes with certainty. He will be loyal to Grant and the band members to a fault. He became an endearing and much-loved employee for many years.

Buzzy's hiring went much better than the search for a housekeeper. As expected, young women and girls soon found out the ad was for Grant, and he was inundated with bogus resumes and phone calls. He got angry at the disgusting and pornographic messages left on his answering machine. He called the newspapers and entertainment magazines to cancel his ad. He hung up on the last interview and heard his doorbell ring. He had not scheduled any new interviews. He peeked out his picture window and saw a middle-aged woman wearing a long black coat. Underneath a bright pink house dress was visible. She had a small felt hat perched on the top of her head that had artificial flowers clustered around the brim. She clutched a black purse in her folded arms. Black sensible shoes were laced onto her sturdy feet. She rang the doorbell again with a purpose. She was not going to give up, so Grant timidly opened the door.

"Yes?" Grant asked her.

"Hi, Mr. Grant I came to start working for you."

"You did?"

"Yup. I have been working for Rod Davis, I'm sure you know him, right? Well, he up and died, and now I need to come and take care of you!" She had no doubt she would be working for Grant.

"Yes, I heard that he passed away. How did you know I was looking for a housekeeper?" He realized that was a stupid question, everyone knew that.

"I do read the papers, Mr. Grant." She sniffed. She pushed on the door, and he automatically moved back to let her in. He figured he'd gone this far; he may as well take her to the kitchen. She was ten steps ahead of him anyway.

He sat down but she looked in his cupboards and refrigerator.

"You just sit down there, Mr. Grant, and I'll fix you a sandwich. You look hungry."

He watched her scooting around in his kitchen like she had been there forever. She sat a huge ham sandwich before him, found a beer in the refrigerator, opened it for him, and sat across from him. He ate.

"I will start next Monday, is that soon enough for you? I must take care of some business that I never had time to do before Rod died. I'm not worried about what you will pay me, because I know it will be great," she said matter-of-factly.

"What's your name?" he asked.

"Oh, it's Matilda Washington. You call me Tillie, that's what everyone calls me."

"Well, Tillie, don't you want to know what the job entails?"

"Mr. Grant, I've been doing this all my life. You don't need to tell me. I've been working for famous guys like you forever, and I know how to keep my mouth shut, and I always will be loyal to you."

He finished his beer while they continued visiting. Grant followed her to the door. He watched her enter her purple Volkswagen, spin it around smartly, and drive away. She came to work on Monday.

Chapter 6

Now was the time for the band to plan their fall tour into the Northwest, ending up in Las Vegas for three nights. They wanted to start in Missoula as they had never played there. Then on to Washington and Oregon and down to Vegas. Buzzy and the manager and accountant began booking venues, transportation and motels. This took several weeks and some setbacks before they approved everything. This also included families, clothes and instruments. They were adding some new songs that were on the newest albums. In September they were ready to roll with the first flight to Missoula for the next Saturday night. Buzzy, as usual, was beside himself with worry, but he functioned perfectly under stress. Everyone came to the airport to see them off, even Tillie came in her Volkswagen. Fans had gotten word that another tour was on, and they crowded the airport with goodbye, good luck and hurry home! There was always a flurry when they boarded a plane. They tried to be congenial and take pictures and sign autographs until the plane departed. The plane arrived in Missoula at one p.m. There was a crowd greeting them. Buzzy capably hurried them and their instruments into a large van limousine and deposited them at their hotel. They were at the venue by 3 p.m. to get set up. They always hired a few roadies to help with the heavy sound boxes, etc. They had time to eat before the show as the opening band wasn't to start until 8 p.m. By 9 p.m. they were dressed and ready to take the stage. The auditorium was full, and the crowd was rowdy and ready for some country music. Now it was their turn! They always opened with Grant's theme song as the curtains opened. The crowd was on its feet stamping, hollering and waving their cowboy hats as Grant came out on the stage waving his. He came to the front and center of the stage and yelled, "Are you ready for some good ole country music?!" The crowd got louder as the band began the theme song again. The show closed with 3 encores.

Bella and Tammy headed for Bella's car in the melee of people and cars trying to leave the show. Both were hoarse from screaming along with the crowd. They decided to sit there for a while and watch the people pushing their cars in front to get away. Finally, Tammy croaked, "Let's stop off for a hamburger and something to drink! Are you comfortable about doing that, or do you want to start home?" "No! That's great! I'm thirsty and hungry and I need to rest to drive home." They found a restaurant off the edge of the highway and pulled in. They ordered their hamburgers and cokes and were getting ready to eat when a commotion began at the door. The Kentuckians entered and shook hands and hugged the women as they wormed their way to a large table in the back. Bella and Tammy were next to them. Lunch was forgotten.

Grant was the last one to sit down. He was right across from Bella. He took off his hat and put it under his chair. He looked up at the girls.

"How are you gals tonight? Out for the evening?"

"We just came from your show!" Tammy chirped.

"Well, what did you think of it?"

"Fantastic!" Bella agreed.

"Where are you kids from?" he continued.

"We live about 30 miles north of here. I'm a nurse and she lives on a ranch!"

Grant tried to get Bella's attention. "What's it like living on a ranch?" Grant looked at Bella expectantly.

Tammy took the hint and sat back in her chair. "Uh, I don't know. I just take care of a lot of the bookwork and take care of my husband and sons."

"I think that's pretty darn important," Grant said. The waitress showed up to take their orders and he turned back to his table.

The girls realized their conversation with him was over. They ate their cold burgers. They stole glances at the band as often as they could. They gathered up their things to leave. Grant turned to them and said, "Have a safe trip home!"

"We will!" gushed Tammy.

"I was wondering if I could write to you and tell you how much I enjoyed the show," Bella bravely said.

"Why, you just do that, little lady," he went along with it.

"Where should I send it?" She was getting her nerve back.

"Just send it to Brentwood. I'll get it, the post office knows where I live." He turned back to his table and promptly forgot about them.

Bella did not. All the way home she kept thinking about him; how his eyes crinkled up in the corners, his hands playing with his hat, how his burnt blonde hair barely touched the top of his jacket. She didn't dare think about other parts of him. She felt her face getting hot. Tammy finally shut up and went to sleep. She woke her up and dropped her off at her place and hurried home. She met one of the cowboys standing watch when she drove in. He said everything was fine and helped her get into the garage. She wished she could have purchased a CD at the show. She drifted off to sleep thinking about one of his new love songs and wished she could remember the words.

Whit and the boys arrived at noon the next day. She ran out to meet them. The boys clambered out of the truck anxious to show her their new things. "Take your stuff into the house, boys. Get washed up for lunch. Bella, get us some lunch," he ordered. "I'll get the calves unloaded and unhook the trailer. Then I'll be in." "Hi, Whit," she said. He glanced at her, surprised. He nodded and drove away.

The boys were anxious to show her their treasures. They got new cowboy hats with big brims, huge belt buckles and leather belts just like dad's. She gasped when she saw their biggest gifts, both boys received .22-gauge rifles.

"Don't worry, Mom, daddy promised to teach us everything before we get to shoot them!" This did not reassure her, and she planned to take it up with Whit later. He came in with a small paper bag decorated with drawings of flowers. He sat it on the counter and said, "Here's a little something for you since you love to cook." She opened it and saw it was indeed another cookbook authored by a local cowgirl cook who was selling her wares at the cattle show. "Thank you," she said and walked over to her desk with the large shelf above that was lined with different cookbooks. She stuffed it in between Betty Crocker and Better Homes and Gardens. She would rather have thrown it at him.

She put together a lunch of roast beef sandwiches, potato salad and strawberries on small cakes with lots of whipped cream. She poured iced tea for her and Whit while the boys had big glasses of milk. They finished their lunch and went out to the pen where the new calves were.

"Why did you buy calves?" She was curious; they usually dealt in heifers.

"They were standing around in a pen and nobody wanted them. The boys went crazy, so I bought them. They must take care of them and play with them. I don't think they are good enough for 4-H." They found a small corral with a shed. Whit got a halter for each boy and let them go to it to put them on the calves and lead them to their new home. Their parents laughed, watching their sons teach the calves how to walk with them. There were times that were good between Bella and Whit.

The week was normal, days turned into new tasks and problems. Bella still did bookkeeping for everyday things, but they had a regular accountant in Missoula that did all the checks and balances. She did her own housekeeping, but once a year they had their home professionally cleaned and painted, if necessary. There were times she would have liked to upgrade but knew not to ask. Tradition at Hamilton's was hard to change. She used all her fantastic cookbooks and made great meals. Whit rarely scolded her about her cooking.

She was thinking about Grant Bartlett much too often. She counted the days that she thought would be appropriate to write to him. When Whit was out on the ranch checking cattle, she sat at her desk and composed several letters she shredded completely. After two weeks she kept one, rewrote it on her private stationery, addressed it and took it to another small town to mail it. She went to the mailbox every day with no response from him. After several weeks with no response, she tried to put him out of her mind unsuccessfully. Just before Thanksgiving, she found an entertainment magazine at the supermarket. She stopped and grabbed onto her shopping cart handle. There he was on the cover! She picked one up and tried not to show her glee. She tossed the groceries into the back seat of the car; they fell off the seat and scattered over the floor and under the front seats. She sat in the back seat, oblivious to the groceries, to stare at his picture. She read the story and sighed with relief. No wonder he hadn't written! He had been on tour and is finishing up a 3-night gig in Las Vegas! He will be back in Nashville soon and will see her letter and will write back! She knew he would!

It took her a while to gather up the groceries. She was huffing, but she felt like singing and dancing around in the kitchen. Whit walked in and stared at her. "What are you doing?" he asked sternly. She quickly thought of a comeback. "Just thinking about Thanksgiving!" "Get me a cup of coffee. I've got some chores to do in the barn. Did you buy any cookies?" She started a fresh pot of coffee and gave him some cookies to munch on. "I plan to start baking tomorrow," "You're not going to ask Mom to fix anything, are you?" He looked at her questioningly. "No, of course not." He gulped his fresh coffee, gobbled the cookies and left for the barn. She poured a cup of coffee and thought about when Sam and Edna decided to move to town.

It was a few years ago. Sam and Whit were planning their yearly trip around the perimeter of the ranch. There were cowboys that did inspections every few days, but Sam wanted he and Whit to do it themselves. They would check fences and ground. Some years they found torn jeans on the barbed wire, even a dead man and a carcass of a horse. A cow or calf was routinely found. They always rode their favorite horse and took a pack horse with a tent and supplies for a couple of nights, if needed. Edna wanted them to take the motor home, but Sam would have none of it. "This is our time to be regular cowboys, just like the Old West!" They got everything loaded on the pack horse and started early one morning. Edna and Bella waved goodbye to them. Edna said she had a bad feeling about this trip. Sam was still in good health, but you never can tell. Bella reassured her, but she, too, felt a little uneasy.

The first day was enjoyable. They had a good time visiting and sharing stories of other rides. Sam was on Blue, his dappled grey gelding with blue eyes. His markings were rare for a quarter horse. Sam loved him and owned him since he was a colt; he broke him himself. It was the same story for Whit; he broke Pete himself, when riding him they were extensions of each other. They brought their favorite pack horse, Henry, who was like part of the family. He went on all excursions like this.

They scouted every inch of the ground and fence and found things going well. They were hoping they could make the trip in two days.

They set up camp by the brook. There was grass and water for the horses and some protection for the campsite. Whit put the tent together and Sam took care of the horses and brought wood for a fire. The supper was cowboy beans and crisp fried bacon with home-made bread made by Edna. Sleep came quickly, as did dawn. They got packed up and began their journey. Whit observed a small rise in the ground with dirt around it, like a burrowing animal would do. He dismounted and gave his reins to Sam. He drew his gun and began to walk towards the mound. He was six feet from the entrance when a large rattlesnake raised his head to see what was going on. Whit fired once and blew the snake's head apart. The gunfire startled Pete. He threw his head up and pulled the reins out of Sam's hand. Blue jumped and Sam slid off his backside and landed on his back and hip.

"Dad!" screamed Whit, "are you okay?" "I don't know, I can't move yet."

"Hang in there, I'll get the horses!" They were quietly drinking water from the brook. He brought them back and tied them up with Henry. He grabbed a whiskey bottle from his saddle bag and ran to his father. Sam still hadn't moved.

"Here, drink this."

"I still can't move," moaned Sam. He took a big swig of the whiskey.

"Dad, I'm going to call 911 and have an ambulance come for you. I'll tell Bella. She knows where we are." Same swallowed another mouthful of whiskey.

"911, what's your emergency?"

"Carol, is that you? This is Whit Hamilton. I need an ambulance at the ranch. Dad fell off his horse and can't move. Stop at the house and pick up Bella. She will know where we are."

"Sure thing, Whit, Brian will be on his way." Carol signed off.

"Bella, Dad fell off Blue and can't move. I called 911 and they are on their way to pick you up. We are at the brook, so you ride with them to show them the way."

"Oh my God! I'll call Edna. Is it bad?"

"I don't know. He can't move."

By the time the ambulance arrived, Sam was quite drunk. Brian asked if that's why he fell off the horse; Whit tried to explain what happened. They carefully loaded Sam into the ambulance and put an oxygen mask on him, mainly to shut him up, but no pain medication, he was feeling no pain right then. He was not injured seriously but was bruised severely. He had a headache the next day.   They kept him a few days for observation. During his recuperation, Sam and Edna had many discussions. They decided to build a small mansion on an acreage on the edge of town. This took several months, and when it was finished, it was a replica of the one on the ranch. They bought new furniture and left the ranch home as it was, to Bella's dismay.

Chapter 7

Grant unlocked his front door and stepped inside. He was happy to be home. He seemed to be more exhausted after every tour but knew he would be ready to go again. This one was exceptionally profitable. His employees received a neat bonus. They would recuperate by working on new songs and doing local gigs.

He took his suitcase into his bedroom and tossed it on the bed. He sat down and worked his boots off. He stuck his legs out and wiggled his toes. He tossed his suit on the floor and took a shower. He put on sweatpants and went to the immaculate kitchen, compliments from Tillie. He appreciated her. He started coffee and saw the huge bag of mail on the floor. He picked it up with his coffee and went to his office. Sipping his coffee, he glared at the bag. "Nope," he said, plopped on his bed and fell asleep. It was still where he left it the next morning.

After breakfast he tackled the mail; one pile for trash, one for bills, and one for fan letters. Trash went in the recycle barrel and bills went in his inbox. Fan mail took the longest. Some he could sign a postcard with his picture, some were run through the shredder, and the rest he had to think about. Bella's letter was in that pile. Those he put on his desk and forgot about. His days of working on old and new songs, lots of jam sessions, and lining up local gigs kept him busy. After two or three weeks he would get to them as his fan base was important to him.

Bella knew when he got back to Nashville. She was beside herself with worry because he didn't write. 'Maybe I should write to him again. No, I'll give him more time.' Every chance she got she would pull the magazine out from its hiding place in her dresser just to look aet him. 'I'm acting like a schoolgirl instead of a married woman!' She looked anyway. Whit had no idea what she was up to.

The Kentuckian's had some shows that required them to take the bus, especially during the holiday season. After the New Year's Eve show, they took off the month of January for much needed rest and relaxation. Grant started working on his fan mail. He was good at typing quick notes on his letterhead stationery, saying thank you and glad you enjoyed the show and watch for when we will be in your area. The small pink envelope slipped out of his grasp. He picked it up and stared at it. When were we in Missoula?' He mused. 'Oh yes, our first show. We ate after the show and I talked to a loud-mouthed blonde that did all the talking, and a little mousy thing scared to talk to me. She said she was going to write, looks like she did.' He opened the letter and began to read. And read it again. 'She is so sad. Lonely too. Something is wrong in her heart.'

He put his stationery into his typewriter. 'Dear (what is her name, she never said,) Bella,' He was going to make it more personal. 'I just read your nice letter today. I have been on tour for the last two months. Thank you for coming to the show. Hopefully, we will get back to the PNW soon. I believe you said you lived on a ranch. What does a girl on a ranch do? You must write to me again and tell me all about yourself. Best regards, Grant Bartlett.' Now why did I write that? I'm asking for trouble. If she's married, I might be asking to get shot again. He left it as is and mailed it, hoping she and her blonde friend would read it and drool over a personal letter from a celebrity and forget about it.

Christmas and New Years came and went. On the first of December, she burned the entertainment magazine and swore she would quit looking for the mail. She accomplished the first. A cold, windy Montana January day began with snow flurries. She saw the mail arrive. She threw on one of Whit's heavy jackets and ran out to the mailbox. She grabbed everything without checking its contents and ran back to the house. Shivering in the kitchen she went through the ads and bills. Suddenly she gasped! She saw his letter. Without checking the rest of the mail, she ran upstairs to her office. Still breathless, she shut the door. Whit, as usual, was out on the ranch somewhere and the school bus wouldn't arrive for several hours. She held his letter with both hands, staring at it. Finally, she took her letter opener and slowly sliced the envelope open. Real words! He wrote real words and not a form letter! She focused on his written words. He wants to know what ranch life is like! He really wants to know! She jumped up and danced around her office. Again breathless, she plopped down in her chair. She had a strong urge to start writing back. No, not yet! I'll wait two weeks. She lasted one.

Whit was going to Missoula for a day. He did not ask her to go with him. This was the day she would write to Grant. She never walked with Whit to his truck to tell him goodbye. He never noticed. She took coffee upstairs, pulled out her stationery and pen and froze. She couldn't think of one sentence! She held the warm coffee mug in both hands. She sipped and the words began to form in her head. Dear Grant, she wrote. After all, he began his letter on a personal note. She felt giddy. Thank you so much for your letter! I had begun to lose hope that you would answer. How nice of you to ask me about ranch life. The words flowed from her pen onto the paper. She did not have to recopy her letter. She asked him what it was like to be a famous person. She wondered if that was too stupid, but she wrote it anyway. She did tell him she was married and had two sons. He needed to know that. She asked him to write to her again. She worded it carefully. He saw right through it. He was right, she needed a friend who was interested in her. He felt compelled to continue writing. He was surprised he felt so strongly. It was a month before he had time to think about his next letter.

The page stayed blank. He twirled a pen between his fingers. What am I doing? He didn't let his thoughts deter him. Dear Bella,

I have been busy recording some new songs. They seem to be stuck in our heads. Being famous is just like any job. Go to work and come home. I just must be more careful when I go someplace. We do have security constantly. He filled her in on a few stories he thought she would enjoy. Paragraph. Tell me about your marriage and your sons. Right now, they are the most important things in your life. He told her about being married to Peggy, but not about Ricky. He finished and sat back in his chair. He wanted to hear from her again.

She opened his letter. She felt as if he had held her close. The things she wanted to tell him tumbled out. She was free to put her thoughts onto paper. She asked him how he felt about love and marriage. He read her letter over and over. They were getting closer with each letter. He wanted to be able to talk to her. He suggested she get her own phone. She took care of household bills; Whit never saw them. She bought the cell phone, and they worked out a schedule when they both were free. Their questions and answers became more personal. They both believed in God. It wasn't safe for him to participate in church services. She was active in hers. Neither one believed in a heavily organized and controlled religion. They belonged to the same political party and felt the country was going in the right direction. They were financially secure and were not afraid to face the future. Their conversations were becoming warmer. They discussed their day-to-day problems with each other and listened for solutions. Waiting for the next call was exciting. Grant was amazed at the changes he felt. He hadn't discussed it with the boys, but they were aware that something special was going on in his personal life. They figured he would tell them sometime. They did know he wasn't dating anyone in Nashville. Nothing was secret in the town. Bella was having a difficult time with the changes in her heart. She had always loved Whit. She did not think he loved her; not completely like she did. As time went on, she knew eventually this thing with Grant had to finish. Yet she wasn't sure of the outcome. They continued with their so-called love affair, looking forward to seeing each other somehow.

"I am thinking about getting another tour together for the PNW. I want to start at Coeur d'Alene, Spokane, then go down into Oregon and end up in Vegas for another 3 nights. Maybe we can see each other for an hour or two in Coeur d'Alene. What do you think?" She was ecstatic! It took several months to get the itinerary completed. The band would fly into Spokane and drive to the large hotel on the lake, have a show, then go back to Spokane. He hoped to see her after they arrived at the hotel. "How will that work?" she asked anxiously. "I know this sounds silly, but I will rent a limousine to drive me across the street. We could meet at the lake." She loved it. She would throw caution to the wind to see him. He wanted to see her too, and knew he was taking a risk. The band would land in Spokane on Thursday morning and be in Coeur d Alene before noon. "Can you be at the lake about 11 AM?" he asked hopefully. "Yes! At the lake!" she promised.

She had one week to get ready. Thousands of thoughts rushed through her head from happiness to guilt. Whit was generally gone into town or out to someone's ranch to inspect new cattle or horses. She was beside herself worrying as he hadn't said anything. Finally, that Wednesday night he told her he was going to meet Greg for lunch. Greg wanted to show Whit the new remodeling he and Tiffany were doing at the ranch. He left that morning without saying goodbye.

She wasn't sure what to do first. She investigated her closet and decided on jeans and a sweater. She carefully put on her makeup, brushed her hair until it shone and fell into its natural curls. Tiny silver buds slid into her earlobes. She glanced into the full-length mirror and decided she looked fine for a woman who was going to meet a man that wasn't her husband. Guilt seeped in, but she pushed it away. She took a light jacket and her purse and walked out the door. Her sporty green car Whit had bought her for a birthday was waiting in the garage. Hopping in, she backed out and gunned it down the long driveway and onto the road, pretending what she was doing was OK. The freeway was before her. She pulled onto it and headed for Coeur d'Alene. Thoughts of her honeymoon ride came to her, and she realized how things had changed since that night. She arrived at the lake at 10:30 and found a parking spot where she could watch the hotel. Needing coffee, she hurried to the concession stand.

"What kind?" asked the young barista.

"What?" She was baffled. "Oh. Latte," she replied as she dug in her purse for some change.

"Gott Cha!" chirped the girl. 'She has no idea what I'm doing here.' She wandered to an empty table and sat where she could see the hotel.

Grant arrived a few minutes before Bella. He went to the band's set of rooms to find Buzzy. "I'm leaving for a few minutes. Don't worry." Buzzy began to worry. Grant went to the consigliere and asked for a limo for a short ride. He went to the VIP entrance and stepped out and into the limousine waiting. "Right across the street to the lake parking lot," he clipped. No request surprised the driver, he had been taking famous people to all sorts of places which he never divulged. He turned in. Grant saw her sitting at the table. "See that woman sitting there? Go get her and bring her here." "Yes, Mr. Bartlett," he promised. He hoped the woman wouldn't be terrified and refuse to come with him to the limo. He removed his cap. "Madam, I need you to come with me to the limousine please. There is a gentleman wanting to see you." Startled, Bella looked at him and at the limo. 'It must be him,' she surmised. He took her arm and led her to the limo. Grant opened the door. She flew into his arms. Grant handed the driver $100 to disappear. He was used to this; he made a lot of extra money that way. Legally, he should not leave the vehicle. Rather than lose the drivers, the hotel simply overlooked it. He sauntered away, but still in range of the car.

Bella fell into his arms and landed on his lap, each hungry for each other. They parted so they could look at each other. She stared into those blue eyes with the crinkly corners, then the mouth she had dreamed about for so long. His arms were wrapped around her so she could not see his hands, but she felt the warmth and strength in them as they caressed her. Grant looked into eyes he had never seen before. They were looking at him with so much love; his heart was moved. He wanted to taste her mouth again. Talking had not started. Grant raised his head. "I've only a few more minutes. We must supervise setting up the stage. Always something goes wrong. Now we know we need to be together." "Yes," she said quietly. "It can never end."

Their time was up. Grant rolled down the window and motioned for the driver. The driver opened the door and escorted her to her table. They drove away. She was exhausted and weak. They loved each other! Now what? She was confused. A park ranger stopped to see if she was ok as he saw she was escorted to her table by the chauffeur. She was embarrassed but told him she was fine and would be leaving soon. The barista in the stand saw this and wondered who she was meeting.

She drove home carefully; freeway traffic buzzed around her and honked. She ran upstairs and threw herself on the bed. Her jacket was too hot. She could smell him on it. Burying her face into the fabric, she inhaled his smell. She thought about washing it but decided to put it deep into her closet. Whit would never know. She changed into her everyday clothes just as Whit arrived. He came into the kitchen yelling for her. "I'm right here!" "Get down here! I want something to eat and coffee. Didn't you bake anything today? I don't see anything." Oh, God! She forgot today was baking day! "Be right there!" She started fresh coffee and made a peanut butter and jelly sandwich. "What the hell is this?" he complained. "Oh, eat it" 'and shut up', she wanted to say.

"Where did you go today?" he asked. How did he know she was gone! "I saw you got the car out." Did he touch the hood to see it was warm? He continued eating. "I was going to go into town but decided not to." That seemed to satisfy him. He slammed his cup down and rose to leave.

"Are you upset about something at Greg's?"

"No! They are fencing in most of the property with high quality fence."

"Why should that bother you? You can refence this whole ranch and pay cash for it."

"It's just he doesn't have to ..." 'He didn't have to sign a contract in order to keep his inheritance like I did.'

"Doesn't have to what?" She was curious.

"Oh, nothing. Send the boys out to the barn when they get home. They need to clean out their calves' stalls." He rammed his hat on his head and stormed out. 'I wonder what he meant by that.' Soon the boys came in yelling for cookies and milk. They, too, got PB&J sandwiches, which was fine with them.

Grant returned to the hotel in time to get lunch at the VIP dining rom. All eyes were on him as he ate. They dared not ask questions. He and Buzzy went to their rooms. Still Grant said nothing. He took a shower and got dressed. He was wearing his gold velvet suit with various colored fake jewels on the collar and down his pant legs. He wore his black boots with rhinestones on the tips. Looking at his reflection in the mirror, he brushed his hair. He didn't bother with makeup. His mind was elsewhere. Swinging his guitar over his shoulder, he took his black hat and put it at a rakish angle. Buzzy was waiting outside. They said nothing on the way to the stage area.

The opening band had set up their instruments and were standing around with the Kentuckians. Everything seemed to be in order, but the band came over to Grant and Buzzy to go over plans one more time. The curtain call came, curtains were opened with a flourish, and the crowd was ready for the show. The opening band finished, lights were dimmed, the MC announced the Kentuckians, and the curtains flew open. Grant's theme song began, and the crowd rose to their feet, stomping and yelling. Grant marched out on the stage, going from one end to the other, staying at least 10 feet from the edge. He had learned early in his career to stay back. He grabbed the microphone and yelled, "Is everybody read for some good old country music?" The crowd got louder, stomping and yelling. Grant removed his hat, turned his guitar around and struck a loud chord. The Kentuckians started his theme song again. Another concert was happening.

It was hard to get away from the adoring crowd. His room seemed blocks but was a long hallway and service elevator away. Buzzy shielded him the best he could. They reached his room shortly. They looked at each other. Buzzy waited until he unlocked the door. "Thanks," said Grant. Buzzy nodded and slipped away. Grant removed his suit and hung it on the valet. He stretched out in the lounge chair and put his hands behind his head. Now he could think about this morning. The fragrance of her hair and the sweetness of her mouth drifted over him. She was like nothing he ever knew. Not Peggy, not Ricky, or any of the other women who crossed his path. For being married, she was naïve and innocent, even when she sat on his lap. He wanted more, but he knew she wasn't able, and he didn't want to push her. He knew they loved each other. Somehow, some way, in time they would be together.

Chapter 8

Bella waited over a year to tell Tammy about Grant. Tammy was thrilled and wanted to know everything. Bella didn't tell her all the precious and special things about their romance, but enough that Tammy knew it was serious. No, Whit had no idea. She had been able to keep it from him, mainly because he wasn't that interested in what Bella thought about or what she did.

Tammy was busy herself. She continued her dating habits, but still was in love with Jeff Silverton, the married hospital administrator. Much to her advantage, Jeff and his wife, Felicity, were having marital troubles. After 17 years of marriage and no kids, they had been discussing divorce. One Sunday morning they were sitting in bed talking. There never was any serious fighting.

"I think I will go to Oregon and see if I can find a nursing job," Felicity opened.

"Oh? Really? Where in Oregon?"

"I don't know. I'll know when I see it. What will you do?"

"I will stay here; you know I like it here. You can take whatever you want or come back and get it later."

"Ok. Sounds good. We'll go see Bernard to start divorce proceedings. I'm going to take a shower, then we will still have time to go to brunch."

"Perfect!" exclaimed Felicity.

The divorce went smoothly. When it was finalized, Jeff helped Felicity load her car, kissed her goodbye, and waved. She gave him the thumbs up and smiled. She found a job in Bend, Oregon in a small hospital as director of nursing. She enjoyed the rain and fragrant pine trees. Jeff was happy for her. The town did their share of gossiping but could come to no conclusion on why they broke up. After a while, it was old news and forgotten. Jeff was settling in on bachelorhood, but decided he was ready to start dating. His first choice was Tammy. He called her into his office and told her to shut the door.

"Tammy, I've known for years you have a crush on me. You know there are no secrets in a hospital. What do you think about a date?"

She sat down across from him. Her dream was coming true!

"When?"

"Saturday night. I'll pick you up at seven."

She left his office in a daze and with expectations. Their dates were bland, mostly dinner dates and movies, or interesting entertainment around town. She was disappointed he didn't want to start a sexual relationship. She did everything she could think of to get him interested. After several months of her trying, he decided it was time to have a talk with her. "Tammy, stop this! I want more from you than sex. I love getting to know you, what you like, what you don't like. How do you feel about nursing, do you like pets and swimming? I want you to get to know me, just me, and not my penis! I am falling in love with you, Tammy, but I want you to decide how you really feel about me."

She began to cry and scooted against the car door. He drove to her house.

"I want you to spend some time to solve this." He didn't walk her to her door, but he waited to make sure she was inside.

Her mother was watching TV. "What in the world happened? Please don't tell me you broke up!"

She sat down on the couch with her mother. Barbara put her arms around her and waited for her to stop sobbing. "He said I had to love more of him than just his penis!" she wailed. Barbara broke into peals of laughter. Tammy was crushed. "Good for him! I was hoping someday a man would come along and love you for you, rather than a romp in the hay. It sounds like he loves you, Tammy. You are receiving a gift. Appreciate it."

She saw him only at work as she studied her dilemma. It took her 2 weeks to grow up and realize what she now had, what she always wanted, but this time it was the whole man.

They planned a fall wedding. Tammy asked Bella to be her matron of honor. Jeff asked a doctor friend to be his best man. Tammy bought a soft, slim gown that blended fall colors into fabric. The reception was in the same restaurant Bella and Whit used. Whit took a minute to wish her well. "It's good to see you finally found a good man after all the others," Whit was being snarky. He could not make himself like her. "Yes, Whit, I had them all but you," she retorted. "And you never will," He smiled and walked away. He found Bella sitting alone at their table. "Come on, let's go home. I've had enough," he demanded. She could see he was upset and wondered what he had done. She gave Tammy a hug, said goodbye to Jeff and they left. They were silent on the way home. Bella went to check on the boys. Whit stayed outside to talk with the cowboy on duty.

She was resting in bed when he came into the bedroom. He got into bed and reached for her. She melted into his arms. He kissed her softly. "My beautiful Bella," he whispered, "I love you." "I love you too, Whit," she answered. He made love to her. Through the years she had learned how to respond. They slept soundly wrapped in each other's arms.

When she woke up the next morning, he was gone. She went downstairs to start breakfast. He was sitting at the computer, busy with the stock market. She made coffee and pancakes. "Better call the boys for breakfast. There's a couple of stalls that need cleaning." Nothing had changed. The boys and Whit left to do chores. Bella sat at the table with another cup of coffee. She wanted to run to her hidden phone upstairs and call Grant. She was filled with emotion and guilt. She knew he would help her through this time and make her feel better.

Several days passed before she could call him.

"Hi, Bella! I'm getting ready to walk out the door to the studio. How are you doing?" She hadn't said a word, so he had no idea the turmoil she was in. People were waiting to help with arrangements for new songs. He was not free to talk.

"Oh, Grant, I did something terrible!"

"What could you possibly do that was so terrible?" He wanted to laugh.

"Whit and I had sex the other night!"

He was surprised but knew not to let her know he thought it was funny, "Well, Bella, honey, of course you had sex with Whit! He is your husband." It never dawned on him to think she wasn't having sex with her husband. He figured it was part of the deal he had to handle.

"I feel so guilty!"

"Why?"

"Because I'm in love with you! It's like cheating on you!"

"No, Bella, it's not! If we were together, then it would be cheating. This is something we don't have to worry about now."

"Are you?"

"Am I what?"

"Having sex?" She was in tears and meant it.

"No"

"Why not?"

"Oh, Bella! I need to go to the studio. I have a crew waiting for me." He hung up. How could he tell her it was killing him to know she was having sex with Whit. He was secretly hoping she wasn't and was pining for him constantly, as he was for her. He was furious with himself, and her. He slammed the kitchen door until it rattled the window. He glanced around to see if anyone was outside. He drove too fast to the studio, daring a cop to stop the great songwriter, Grant Bartlett. He pushed the studio door open. They stared at him as he sat down breathless at the piano. The session did not go well that day.

Chapter 9

Jeremy was graduation from high school. Whit was not happy with his choice for a career. He signed up for the Marines during a military recruiting day at high school. All branches of the military were invited. They arrived in their dress uniforms. They were polished and handsome and anxious to recruit. Jeremy was most impressed with the Marine sergeant. His dress blues were impeccable. He was standing at parade rest observing the kids. He noticed Jeremy staring at him. He marched over to him.

"Come over to my table, son," he commanded. Brian Stewart had been in the Marine corps for over 20 years. He had seen combat and had been injured. Now he was done fighting. He had this new deployment. He loved talking to the kids, making them enthused and anxious to serve their country. He knew all the ploys and benefits to offer, and he was good at it. He also had a quota to fill. He took Jeremy by the shoulder to his table. Jeremy couldn't take his eyes off Brian. He listened intently and Brian handed him the application. He signed it. But he wasn't 18 yet and would need his parents' signatures. Jeremy's shoulders slumped, but Brian said don't worry, he had 2 months to convince his parents to sign, and if they didn't, he was free to choose on his own. He took the application home and was not surprised at the reaction from his father.

"No way are you going in the service!" Whit fumed. "You are going to the university just like I did, get your degree, and come home to run the ranch!"

"No, I am not! There are other things I want to do with my life!"

"What is better than ranching?" Whit continued storming.

"I want to travel and make the world a better place!" he countered.

"By taking a gun and killing people?"

"No, dad. There are so many opportunities in the Marines to protect the environment."

"You just got tangled up with all the recruitment big talk! You are going to college!"

This went on for weeks. He turned 18 and Brian came out to the ranch to finalize the application without his parents' signatures. He arrived in a polished government vehicle and stepped out in his dress blues. Jeremy's heart jumped into his throat, and he knew he was making the right decision. Brian sat with Whit and Bella at the kitchen table and gave the same story he gave Jeremy. Whit was not impressed. Bella was in tears.

"Dad! Grandpa Archer was in the Army and in Viet Nam!"

"So?"

Brian had enough. He pulled out the papers and Jeremy signed them. In a few weeks he came to get their son, this time wearing camo. Bella was in tears and Whit put on a brave front. He hugged his eldest son and stood back as Jeremy got in the vehicle. Brian shook Whit's hand and hugged Bella. He understood what they were going through. Basic training in San Diego went by swiftly. Before they knew it, they were at Missoula to welcome him home. He had time off, TDY was next. There were several servicemen exiting the plane. "They all look alike!" exclaimed Bella. A young man came towards them. He was over 6 feet tall with bulging arms under his camos. His cap was pulled over his eyes military style.

"Mom!" he yelled and easily picked her up and swung her around. "Dad!" he reached for Whit's hand but decided to pick him up also. When he put Whit down, he towered over his father. "Let's go get my duffel bag off the carrier. I can hardly wait to see Jesse!" They obediently followed, still speechless. Jesse couldn't believe his brother had changed. He was bursting with pride! The family enjoyed their time together, but soon Jeremy was restless and ready for TDY. They took a grown man to the airport this time.

Two years later, Jesse was graduating in the spring. He had no problem with his father. He would register for the fall term at MU, paid in full by Whit. Jesse was planning on many of the same classes as Whit. He wondered if he would learn anything more than what his father had but didn't question it. He was happy to do what Whit wanted. He, too, devoted his life to the ranch and wanted nothing more. He picked a few elective courses such as weather and climate changes and geology. Someday he would like to see if there was oil somewhere on the ranch. He will be 18 in August. His life was perfect.

Whit planned to buy a horse for Jesse's graduation and birthday. He kept hinting to Jesse about what kind of horse he would like. "Oh, Dad, I have the pick of the horses here," and offered no suggestions.   Whit had made up his mind he was going to purchase one. For months he had been scouring horse sales all over the United States. He chose Temecula, California. For once, he discussed this with Bella and asked her to go along. She was excited about seeing California, she didn't care where. They planned to leave on the first of October when Jesse would be home on break from the university. Jesse thought it was great his folks were going away. Whit wanted to take the new pickup and horse trailer in case he bought a horse. Jesse didn't question it; Dad could be looking at cattle.

In Nashville, Grant and the Kentuckians had been pouring over a new tour. They were going to hit California, Arizona and Las Vegas. They were starting at Temecula on the first of October. Grant hadn't discussed it with Bella until he was sure of the dates.

Bella called him to tell him about her trip.

"Grant! I'm going to California! Well, Whit and me. I told you he has been shopping for a horse for Jesse. He decided on Temecula on the first of October. Have you ever heard of that?" Silence. "Grant, have you ev."

"Oh, Bella!" He stopped.

"Grant?"

"Are you ready for this? We open the tour there the first of October!"

Now it was her turn to be speechless. "Do you think?"

"I don't know! Do we dare?"

Their thoughts and voices returned. They spent what seemed like hours planning how they could meet. Finally, they decided they would have to wait until the day they both were there. Grant would land in San Diego and the crew would do as they did in Coeur d' Alene. After the show they would come back to San Diego for the show there the next day. Their meeting would again be brief, but they wanted to grab whatever they could. Bella and Whit arrived first. Whit found a hotel close to the horse venues. There were several he could attend. He was able to park the horse trailer in a special parking lot provided for both sellers and buyers. The hotel was elegant and designed for busy horse traders. The lush grounds melted into a small park frequented by dog walkers and joggers. Dirt paths wandered in and out among trees and cement tables and benches. A small parking lot for visitors was available. After Whit got her settled into their suite, he left to look at several venues and stalls.

She sat on the luxurious bed and kicked off her shoes. She started to giggle and jumped on the bed and tried to bounce up and down. She fell into a mound of fluffy pillows and berated herself for being so childish. She rested while waiting for Grant's call. Her special phone rang.

"Grant!"

"Yes. I have directions to the hotel. Where will you be?"

"There is a small park behind the grounds of the hotel. I will be waiting!"

"Ok Bella, I'll be there soon." They hung up.

She put her phone in her purse. Suddenly Whit burst into the room. "Come on Bella! We are going to lunch with the seller and his wife! Then we can look at campers!" He was almost dancing with glee. A thousand thoughts raced through her mind. She turned away from him and rubbed an eye.

"Oh, Whit, I can't go! I developed a sinus headache! My eye is swelled up and I feel terrible.!" She turned around so he could see the red eye she caused.

"Put some makeup on it and let's go!" He was exasperated with her.

"No!" She stood her ground. He looked at her with disgust and left.

She went to the lavatory and put cold water on her eye, which helped. She waited for a while to make sure he didn't storm in demanding that she goes. No return.

She picked up a light sweater and her purse and gingerly peeked out. All was clear. She entered the elevator, went through the lobby and out into the luscious grounds. She ran across the grass and wondered if someone would yell at her to get off. Suddenly she was in the park area. She sat on a bench to wait for him. Two young women were jogging on the dirt path. An old pickup pulled into a parking spot. A middle-aged man got out. He wore old jeans, tennis shoes, and a grey sweatshirt. A baseball cap was pulled low over his eyes. Bella observed him and put her purse closer to her and was ready to run. He started walking rapidly toward her. She was frightened and began walking away from him.

"Bella!" He yelled. She stopped dead and turned towards him. They ran to each other. Their arms locked and no words were spoken. They parted and looked at each other. "Come to the truck," he said. With arms around each other they got to the truck. Grant opened the door, and she climbed in. He closed the door and went around the truck and got in the driver's side and slid down in the seat. She leaned over to touch his leg. Just then, the women jogged by.

"Get a room!" one offered. They laughed and kept jogging.

"God, I can't do this again! This could ruin me. I do not want to be away from you anymore, Bella. It's up to you. I am not tied down to anyone. I don't want to be impatient with you. We have a beautiful relationship that needs to be fulfilled."

She leaned against the door brokenhearted. He was right, but it still hurt. These meetings were not enough and left them frustrated. She was the one to make the decision. She was going through the turmoil of every woman who wants to leave her husband for another man. This was more complicated since Grant was famous. She did not want to be the ruination of his career.

"You are completely right, Grant. It's all up to me."

"I'm so sorry, Bella," is all he could offer.

She got out of the truck. They looked at each other with sorrow in their eyes. She turned away and went to the hotel.

Grant watched her go. He did not plan to forget her, but something had to be done. He would give her a while to decide what to do. He drove the pickup back to the car rental and rode to the venue in a limousine he had hired. He entered by the stage entrance. Buzzy was waiting for him. "Grant, are you ok?" "Yes, Buzzy. Help me get to my dressing room." Buzzy delivered him and said he would be back in time so he could be on stage for the inspection.

Grant wadded up his chore clothes and stuffed them in his duffel bag. He took a shower and was ready when Buzzy came for him.

The routine started as always; the lights dimmed, the band played his theme song, he made his entrance, and the show was under way. It was a glorious night for the Kentuckians. The crowd wanted encore after encore.

There were two couples in the nosebleed section that were having a good time. During a lull in the music and noise, one girl looked at her friend and said," You remember that couple we saw in the park today and I told them to get a room?" "Yah, so what?" "Well, I thought that guy looked well groomed. I noticed how his golden hair was trimmed along his neckline. He was no bum. He was Grant Bartlett!" "Oh Geez, you think so?" She watched him move on stage. "Yup, you're right! Wouldn't he be taking a terrible chance doing that?" They laughed and wondered who the woman was.

Bella returned to their room and sat on the edge of the bed. She wiped tears from her eyes. She thought about taking a nap but knew that was impossible. Whit burst into the room causing her to jump.

"Bella! Come on! Get up! Has your headache gone? I guess not, both eyes are red and swollen. Take some pills. We are going to the RV place I saw and pick out a small camper for the pickup bed. I bought the horse!" He was breathless with excitement.

"Why do I have to go?"

"Because I want you to! Now, wash your face or something and put some lipstick on! Hurry up!" Bella thought at times like this she could come up with an answer to leave him. Rather than argue, she did as she was told.

"Tomorrow, we pick up the horse at 8 am and will be on our way home. I signed the papers. I'll have Hollingsworth get the papers ready and sent. She has a pedigree! But she has been fixed, she's for Jesse's enjoyment and not for breeding."

"Uh huh," mumbled Bella, trying to remember everything. Grant's face kept popping up while Whit talked.

The RV people were happy to oblige this very rich man and his sad wife. Whit picked out a camper, but she didn't go inside, she said that's fine and returned to the pickup. She had to go into the showroom while they mounted it, filled it with water and propane, and made sure all amenities were working properly. They removed the pickup tail gate and promised to ship it to Montana. Whit wrote a check for all of it. They knew not to insult him by asking for ID. "That is one sad lady, and I don't think she is looking forward to sleeping in that tonight!" The owner mused. They shook their heads, then laughed all the way to the bank.

"Now we are going to stop at the grocery store for coffee, rolls, lunch meat, etc., just to get home. I don't expect you to cook." He thought she would appreciate that and was proud of himself for saying it. She ignored him. He made her pick out the groceries.

Together they put the things in the new camper. Then he hit her with another bombshell.

"We are going to dinner with John and Camille tonight."

"Who?"

"The couple that owned the horse."

"I thought you went to lunch with him!"

"It was just a quick one, then we went to see the horse."

"I didn't bring any evening clothes," she said with confidence, hoping it would get her out of dinner. It did not. He informed her that this is California cowboy country, and anything goes.

Somehow, she got dressed in what she brought. She wore a light grey cashmere sweater with dolman sleeves. Her Levis fitted her perfectly. Grey cowgirl boots completed her wardrobe. A silver choker necklace and long silver slits in her ears finished her outfit. Whit noticed how gorgeous she looked. He tried to kiss her neck, but she turned away. 'Why do I ever try to please her, it's a waste of time. It's probably too late after all the years I have let slip by.' He tried anyway. "Come on, you gorgeous thing, let's go wow them! Maybe he will buy dinner and I will only have to tip!" She rewarded him with a small smile.

John and Camille were sitting at the bar having cocktails. John wore a tailored western suit with a crisp white fitted western shirt open at the collar. His hand-made boots were of finest black leather with elaborate stitching. Camille had on a cream-colored western suit with an open jacket. A peach-colored tank top with a plunging neckline showed her flawless skin and ample bosom. She wore huge turquoise jewelry everywhere possible. John came to meet them and took them to the bar. "Can I offer you cocktails before dinner?" "Yes, of course. I will have bourbon on the rocks, and Bella will have a Cosmo." 'What in the hell is a Cosmo?' Bella wondered but dared not suggest something else. That would be criticizing Whit. They visited until their table was ready. Bella enjoyed sipping the drink and found it relaxed her. She enjoyed the conversation with these different people. They left several hours later as friends. Whit invited them to come to the ranch any time.

The next morning, they arrived at the barn to collect Jesse's new horse. John had a groomer bring the mare outside to walk her. He was brushing her coat until it shone. Whit got his halter and lead out of the trailer and approached her. She watched him and nickered as he removed her old halter and put on his. He took the blanket he brought and let her smell it, then he gently put it over her back. He led her to the trailer and stopped so she could inspect it. Satisfied, she hopped in on her own. Whit slid into the front and fastened her lead on the ring. He quietly shut the doors and bolted it. She made no fuss. Whit was a fine horseman; he loved them as much as his cattle.

He reached in to start the truck so she could feel the engine running. He shook John's hand and nodded to Camille. Bella said goodbye to John and she and Camille exchanged a quick hug, then she got into the truck. No one wanted to say anything. They waved and Whit and Bella were gone. "I think we made a good sale; don't you think so?" "Yes, I do. I think we should try to go to Montana sometime." "Yes, of course."

Jesse was waiting as they drove in. "Hi you guys! What have you brought home now?" He was surprised to see it was a horse. "Dad! Why did you get another horse?"

Whit got out of the truck and hugged his son. Bella did the same. Love was radiating around these people. Jesse opened the trailer doors. Whit said, "Go ahead easy and unhook her and bring her out!" He did as gently as his father. She backed out and stopped to look at Jesse and smell him.

"Are you going to breed quarter horses now, Dad?"

"No, Jesses. She's fixed."

"Well, then, what the heck?"

"I bought her for you, Jesse. For your graduation and 18th birthday. You need a reason to come home during breaks at school. She is yours to have fun with as long as she lives."

For a minute, Jesse buried his face in her neck and mane. He began to cry and reached for his mother and father in a bear hug. He said, "Thank you. Her name is Queen."

For the next four years he did just that. He graduated with honors and came home anyway. He was like his father; he loved the land and all its inhabitants.

Chapter 10

Grant was happy to be home. He was tired and his knees were hurting, especially when he was traipsing around on the stage. He had put on some weight and found it was hard to swing his guitar around over his head. To top it all off, one time he forgot to take his hat off. He wanted to leave the stage over that one, but the boys made it look like it was part of the act. The tour had been successful, but by the time they finished the 3-night show in Vegas, he was exhausted. Seeing Bella for that short period had been frustrating. He had to end trying to meet like that. She understood, but he could see it was breaking her heart. He did not contact her during the tour. He wanted her to try and decide. He was going to call her after he was settled at home.

Tillie was in the kitchen with flour up to her elbows. She had been baking pies all morning as she knew Grant would be home at any time.

"Hi Tillie! Wow, that smells good! Is it pies?"

"Of course, Mr. Grant, your favorite chocolate is cooling, and this one is chocolate mousse. Cut you a piece?"

"Let me put my things in my bedroom and take a shower. I'd love coffee with that pie."

He deposited everything on the floor, took a shower, put on a sweat suit and flip flops. He padded to the kitchen and sat down to a huge piece of chocolate pie with a mountain of home-made whipped cream on top.

"You trying to get me fat so I can't work anymore?" He chided.

"No, Mr. Grant, I just love to see you eat!"

She poured herself a cup of coffee and sat down to talk with him. She informed him of the news in the neighborhood. He finished his dessert and returned to his bedroom.

His fancy outfits were going to the cleaners. He noticed how sweat soaked they were. He removed his work clothes from the duffel bag. He picked up the sweatshirt he was wearing when he was with Bella. He held it to his nose and could still smell her fragrance. He felt her mouth on his as if she were here with him now. Her hands were searching his body, but stopped before they went too far. He longed to finish what they started. He tossed them in the laundry pile. He sat for a while remembering. "Stop it!" He berated himself and went to his office and began going through the usual pile of mail. He was bored, so he made a list of things to discuss with the guys and business partners.

The thing that was bothering him the most was the clothes they had worn for years. The band had several pairs of black pants. The black shirts had fancy white scrolls across the chest. They had black jackets but didn't always wear them. He didn't think boots would be a problem. He always wore one of his elaborate suits. He observed the opening bands and usually was appalled at what they were wearing; mostly jeans worn low on the hips and stretched out tee shirts. Some wore tennis shoes. It didn't seem to bother the fans, but it disgusted him. The band had never suggested they change. He planned to bring it up to everyone. It would involve money for new outfits.

He had the same guys since they started, except for Huey, early in their careers. They were getting older, some had health problems, but hadn't inferred with playing, so he didn't feel afraid to bring up this next problem. He wanted to have his guitar on a stand when he came onto the stage, due to his fiasco on tour. This interruption could cause some time interference with the theme song. He wondered what they would think if he did not wave his hat, but just come out and get his guitar. He hated to admit these problems were due to his age.

In his heart, he knew he did not want to go on long tours anymore. The money was fabulous, so this will take a long discussion. He sighed and went back to his mail.

Two weeks later, a meeting was scheduled in the conference room of Herb Ellers, their attorney. He catered lunch and drinks for Grant and his employees. They sat at a round polished, mahogany table which gleamed and the glass covering was spotless. Executive chairs were deep and comfortable. Everyone felt relaxed as Grant took charge.

"You have had a chance to read the three changes I want to discuss. I have explained thoroughly my thoughts on each matter. Let's start with the first." They continued with the second and third problems. They agreed with the first two, but they weren't' sure about giving up the tours because the money was so good. The decision was made to try smaller shows in surrounding states for eight months. If it wasn't profitable, they would go back on tour. Albums wouldn't sell as well since they were not going all over the states. He felt the same dilemma too, but in his heart, he didn't want to go. He had always realized that he was responsible for their paychecks and if he didn't work, they didn't make money. He didn't feel animosity among the group after the meeting. The band wanted to go for drinks, but Grant declined. He was exhausted and wanted to go home.

The meeting was transcribed and put into a bound folder. The new clothes were ordered. Everyone was pleased with them, including the accountant who wrote checks for them. The band practiced the new moves before they had a show. Grant felt much better physically. After their first show, they received some gaffes from fans, but it didn't last long. Grant experimented with writing a few songs in the new genre. The boys tried to get the rhythms right and match the words accordingly. It did not work. Grant changed his songs back to his old ways. They put the new songs on an album and released it without much fanfare. It did well locally, but, as they were afraid of, it did not make it on a billboard or in the top ten. They could not help feeling discouraged. Grant felt some rumblings among them. Nothing was going well, and he was depressed.

He knew he had to talk to Bella. They had always been able to talk about their problems. He never called her since they saw each other. He didn't want to discuss that issue; he wanted to tell her about his dilemma. She kept her phone off all the time until she called him. It went to voice mail. But a few minutes later she called.

"Bella."

"Grant."

Silence.

"I need to talk to you about what's going on here." She panicked.

"Are you OK?"

"I'm not sick." She sighed audibly through the phone.

"I need to tell you about work. Can you talk for a while?"

"Yes."

He told her the long story, leaving nothing out. She was heartsick and wanted to be with him to comfort him throughout his story.

"Are you wanting to retire?" she offered. He was stunned. He had not thought of that.

"I don't know! I'll have to think about it. See, I knew I needed to talk to you, not just wondering if you decided yet. I may as well ask, have you?"

"My decision is to leave, but I can't. You and I are in a mess, Grant. I should break up with you, but I love you too much. Do you love me enough to just go on, or do you want to leave?"

"No." He rubbed his eyes and ran his fingers through his hair. Still no answer there, but she gave him a new perspective to mull over.

"Grant? Are you still there?"

"Of course. Let me get back to you after I think about the idea of retiring. I am like you; I can't just quit. All my employees depend on me. Oh, Bella, I love you honey! Bye now!"

He hung up before she could answer. She did anyway to a dead phone: "I love you too, Grant." At least he had something new while her problem was the same.

He continued to be stressed. He didn't talk to Tillie when he came home. She missed their visits and baking his favorite pies. He lost the weight he had gained. She cornered him one evening when he came home.

"Mr. Grant, I want to talk to you." She had baked chocolate pies to bribe him.

"Oh, God, tell me you are not quitting! I've got enough problems without that! I'm sorry, Tillie, had no business yelling at you."

"No, of course not. But you need something to come home to." She dished up a huge piece of pie and whipped cream. She poured coffee for them and sat across the table from him.

"You need a dog." He had a piece of pie in his mouth. He gagged and laughed at the same time. Tille jumped up to get him a glass of water.

"Oh, Tillie!" he whispered, unable to swallow the pie yet. He drank the water and continued. "I can't get a dog! What would it do here by itself all day when we aren't here? No, it wouldn't be fair to the dog. But thanks anyway,"

"Well then, get a cat. I'm not particularly fond of them, but if it helped you…."

"Nope."

"But you can leave them alone longer than a dog."

"Tillie, stop it! But you have made me feel better for a while and I really loved the pie!"

Sometimes Grant liked to go to the supermarket at one or two in the morning, so he didn't run across so many fans. That night he stepped out of the car, looked around and saw nobody. He looked down by the returned carts and saw a small orange kitten huddled against a cart. "What are you doing out here in the middle of the night? Where is your mother?" The kitten ran to him and brushed his leg. "Go home now," he said and walked away. The kitten went back to the cart. Grant entered the store. "Hi, Mr. Bartlett!" The young clerk knew he was a frequent customer. "Hi, Paul." He took a cart and started down an aisle. By then the few customers in the store came over to him as they heard Paul's greeting. Grant stopped for a minute and signed autographs. They left him alone. He picked up what he needed, and Paul checked him out. "Let me take the groceries for you, Mr. Bartlett," he offered. They walked out together. Grant opened the rear door and Paul put the groceries on the seat. The orange kitten ran to the door and into the front seat. It immediately curled up and went to sleep. "Let me get him for you." "No, just leave him. I'll take care of it." He gave Paul $10.00. "Gee thanks! I'm not supposed to take it," hemmed Paul. "Go ahead, I'll never tell." Paul whistled as he ran back to the store with the empty cart.

Grant got in the car and looked at the sleeping kitten. It opened its eyes, then hopped on Grant's leg and started making biscuits and purring loudly. "Ow! That hurts!" scolded Grant. The kitten went back to the seat and curled up again and went to sleep. Grant looked at the kitten again. He saw a pet supply store in the same complex as the grocery store. He drove there.

He entered and was loudly greeted by four employees cleaning up to close. He went through the same routine as the grocery store, greeting the clerks. "I have a kitten and need to buy everything for it." "I'll help you," Trace the assistant manager said importantly. He took Grant into the cat department and loaded his cart with everything imaginable for a kitten. "Do I really need all this stuff?" Grant asked dubiously. "Yes! From kitten food to litter box! Your new kitten will be living in style!" "Ok." Grant bought it all. Trace carried it out for him. Grant found another $10.00 and gave it to Trace. "Gee thanks, Mr. Bartlett!" He made no apology for taking it. Grant put the kitten in its brand-new carrier. He left it in the car as he unloaded his groceries and kitten paraphernalia. He was afraid it would run away, especially after he just bought over $200.00 on the finest products a kitten could have. 'What am I doing, you are a crazy old man,' he chided himself. He put the groceries away and fixed up the kitten's new home. He let it out of the carrier, and it went to the litter box, then its food. Grant watched it with enjoyment. He picked it up and petted it. He discovered it was a boy. "Okay, guy! Your name will be Jake!" This caused Jake to purr louder. Grant took him to the vet to be sure he was healthy, spent another $400, and took his manhood away, which didn't seem to bother him. Grant and Tillie loved him but wouldn't admit it.

Chapter 11

Eight months arrived. The band got together in the studio to decide what to do. There was only one answer; they needed to go back on tour to keep the money rolling in. Grant had the accountant print out everything from the last eight months. They did well at first, but towards the end, it was slipping. The problem was they kept returning to the same venues and the fans were getting used to seeing them. It was no longer special.

Ever since Bella asked him about retiring, he couldn't stop thinking about it. He wondered if the guys ever thought about retiring. He was going to bring it up now. He cleared his throat.

"I guess it's evident that we need to go back on the road. We are all over 60, except Huey. I have provided a good retirement program for my employees. I will be honest with you. I am tired. I want to make this our final tour; go out while we are still on top."

"Is your girlfriend finally free, is that what you are thinking?" Rick asked sarcastically. 'How did he know that?' He thought how nothing is safe in Nashville. The other members gasped. Grant stood up. His hands were clenching and unclenching at his sides. Rick stood up. "Since you made this your business, I will answer with one word, no. Does anyone else have a question before we continue?" No one did. Rick sat down. Something just died between Grant and Rick. He was sorry for what he asked. Grant put his hands together and began again.

"We can choose our favorite cities and close again at Vegas with three nights. I don't want to make hasty decisions until we all agree. Does anyone want to walk out now?" He looked at Rick. There was no comment.

"Okay. We will plan the details after we work out a mutual agreement between us." They left silently. He just told them their careers as the Kentuckians were over. He was surprised he did it. They will do fine, either stay retired or find another band. The phone rang. It was Buzzy. Someone had called him. It probably was Rick.

"Hi Grant. Are you OK? So, you did it! I'm proud of you. It's time. They will come around. You need anything?"

"No, Buzzy. We will schedule another meeting at Herb's and see how bad the "excrement" hits the fan!" They laughed.

He sat in his car and thought of the magnitude of what he had done. His career was over, just like theirs, and he was stunned, but happy. He hoped Bella didn't have her phone shut off. He tried. She did. He went home to wait for her call.

"Grant! It's been so long!"

"Bella, I did it! I told the band I was retiring, and this was the end of the Kentuckians!" They talked about the changes as long as they could. Bella was as excited as Grant was. How she wished she could be with him! "I will let you know when it's settled. If they want, we will do the farewell tour." She did not want to leave him, but this was as long as she was free. He sat in his recliner taking in all that happened that day. He, too, wished she were here with him.

It took more than one day to resolve everything. All involved chose what town and what venue, and music. This plan took several months, as always. The venues were sorry to hear this was their last tour. It was beneficial to both parties. They chose all their favorite songs but did use a few from the last album that didn't sell well. Rick found a new job as a backup singer and guitarist with a hot new young guy who was climbing up the billboards and charts. He never told Grant; he knew he would be disappointed with the music and dress code. He would stay for the tour as he was under contract. He had lost the comradery of his fellow bandsmen and Grant.

Plans were finalized and the tour would start in the spring. They still played local shows until then. The crowd demanded the old songs, so they obliged most of the time. It was fun but bittersweet for the band. Grant's business crew was busy finalizing or adding or correcting the large amount of paperwork to dissolve the company. Several had been together since the start, or added on as the company grew. They were familiar with the Nashville music situation and realized things sometimes came to an end. Grant loved them all and made sure they were taken care of.

The tour started May 1. They arrived at the airport and saw the large crowd waving; some were waving flags. Police were there holding back the excited throng. Some were against them leaving and had signs saying, 'don't quit' and 'no way'. Security helped them board the plane. Grant was the last one boarding. Buzzy blocked him from entering the plane. He let Grant turn around and wave his arms high in a final gesture to his fans. Buzzy led him to his seat with the rest of the crew in first class. Grant had tears in his eyes and wiped them away. Rick looked out the window and watched the crowd disperse. They sat with their eyes down, engrossed in their own thoughts. The flight attendant offered drinks. They landed at Omaha. This was the first time there and they were playing at Ak-Sar-Ben, a huge venue that hosted many famous singers and other entertainers. They were excited about their performance that night. Grant wasn't sure how full it was, but by the sounds of the fans, it was packed. It helped after the bittersweet goodbye at Nashville airport.

They went to Kansas City, Oklahoma City, down to Albuquerque, Tucson and Phoenix. They hit a few of the smaller towns along the way. Phoenix was getting hot by now, but this was scheduled for a few days off before they hit Vegas. They had a fabulous resort with all kinds of amenities, including 2-3 swimming pools, one with a bar they enjoyed. They were used to nice accommodations, this wasn't new to them, but was relaxing. They were getting older, and they found they enjoyed the spas and massages, plus the abundance of Mexican food. They wouldn't admit it, but they did a lot of sleeping.

The quick early morning flight got them to Vegas by noon. The first show was that night, and they were ready for a great show for their Vegas fans. They were at the same casino venue they always used. The auditorium was always packed when they came, and tonight was no exception. Their clothing and opening were different, but the crowd didn't seem to mind. They were yelling, stomping and clapping as usual. Grant wondered if they would fill it up for two more nights. They did, and it was magical. Encore after encore went on until Grant had to stop it. They were ushered out the stage door by security into their limousine.

Grant asked the driver to take them to a small hide-a-way where they could get drinks and food. He knew just the place. He quietly took them through a small back door used for just this purpose. The manager greeted them and took them to a table in an available corner. Grant looked around to see if he knew anyone. He didn't because it was so dark. They ordered drinks from a waitress that they were not sure if she had clothes on. They ate and drank. The boys ended up at the bar or at the few slot machines. Grant was alone, lost in his own thoughts. A woman a little younger than Grant came up to him.

"Care if I sit down?" she asked quietly.

"Huh?"

"I asked you if you cared if I sat down."

"All the seats full?" Questioned Grant groggily.

"No. I want to sit with you. You seem sad."

"No, I'm not sad."

"Well, let's see if you are."

"Why would you care if I'm sad?" he asked belligerently.

"I'm sad too. We can keep each other company." She sat down and ordered a drink. She looked at him through heavily made-up eyes. Her black hair was piled on top of her head. She twisted a strand that was drooping off her forehead. Her makeup was beginning to look caked, but her lips were still bright red. Cheap earrings dangled from her ears. She had little more clothes on than the bar maid. She tried another angle.

"Are you lonely as I am?"

"I'm not lonely, either."

"Let's see how lonely you are."

Huey was at the bar. He saw what she was doing. He quickly rounded up the others. "Before we interrupt, let's see what she does!" They stood by the bar and watched.

She had no idea who she was talking to. She rubbed his shoulder and moved her hand down to his leg. Grant came alive and jumped up so fast his chair went flying.

"Get the hell away from me! Get those grimy fingers off me!"

"You probably were a cheap trick anyway!" She glared at him and walked to the bar. Laughing, the guys made room for her. Grant steadied himself and the guys came over to him. They were proud of him, but he was humiliated. They left a huge tip for the waitress and manager and went outside to the waiting Limo.

Grant was troubled by what happened. Of course, he had been propositioned many times throughout his career. After indulging in what the ladies had to offer, he learned to blow them off. He was amazed at some of the offers, young girls, older women, even guys. After Bella claimed his heart, he walked away without acknowledging them. Last night was a fluke. During his stay in Phoenix, he did much soul searching. When he got home, he was going to tell her this had to end. Her kids were grown, Jeremy had a career in the Marines, Jesse graduated and was home with Whit. He could take care of Whit. He couldn't think what was holding her back.

He would find something to do that he was unable to do because of the years on the stage. Maybe golf. He could think of nothing else. Writing songs and singing them had been his whole life for over 40 years. 'Ah, I'll deal with it,' he assured himself. It all looked deep and boring. Another love was out of the question. 'Guess it will be just me and Jake,' he wallowed in despair. Last night's ending was too much! He wished he had not suggested the restaurant.

The next morning, they boarded the plane home to Nashville. Word got out they were arriving. There was a smaller crowd this time. The Kentuckians had SUV's waiting for them on the tarmac and Buzzy supervised them entering the dark windowed van. They sped away and were delivered to their homes. They would be meeting with Herb again in a few weeks. No one said anything. They did not realize this would be so hard.

A group of people were standing on the lawn and sidewalk at Grant's house. The driver pulled up to his back gate. For once, he wished there was security. He was exhausted and felt sick. Buzzy wasn't with him. Grant asked the driver to unlock the back gate and drive in, then close it. He was willing to help. Grant stayed in the van. People banged on the gate, wanting to see him.

"I'm calling 911. I need help."

"Yes, of course, Mr. Bartlett. Stay in the van until we get there." They were there in five minutes and cleared the crowd. They helped with the luggage and guided him to his door. Tillie opened the door.

She was terrified and couldn't manage to call 911. She was crying hysterically.

"Oh, Mr. Grant, I am so sorry! I was scared to death!"

"That's OK, Tillie, I'm here now and it will be fine." He turned to the policemen.

"Thank you, boys. I'm getting too old for this!"

"Any time Mr. Bartlett." They tipped their hats and left.

"Oh, God, Tillie, I am exhausted. I'm going to my bedroom. Will you be ok? Don't worry about anything, just rest."

"Yes, I'll go down to my room and later I'll fix something to eat."

She never did. The Bartlett house was dark until morning.

The first month of retirement was great. Grant didn't shave and wore sweatpants every day. He tinkered in his back yard and debated on painting the fence. The other Kentuckians did the "honey do" requests, played with their kids and went to their school functions. By then, the women were tired of them underfoot, even Tillie, who, of course, couldn't complain since she worked for Grant. Rick had not taken the new job. One day he got in touch with the rest of the guys, except Grant.

"I can't do this anymore. Have you heard if the studio is still open?" No one had.

"What do you say we go in there next Monday morning and do some jamming?" To the girls' relief, they decided to do that without checking with Grant. That same Monday morning he told Tillie he was going to the studio and see what kind of shape it was in. He had cancelled the cleaning crew. It smelled of old food and being shut up. He picked up the trash and hauled it to the dumpster. He sat down at the piano looking at sheet music he had started working on several months ago. He played a few notes, then sat thinking. Suddenly the door opened, and the guys came in.

"Grant! We didn't know you were here. What are you doing?"

"I could ask you the same thing," he retorted.

"We decided to come in and play around with some songs."

"That's what I'm doing. I am going nuts at home!"

"So are we! My wife is ready to kick me out!" They agreed with laughter.

They played until noon, then went to lunch. At 4 o'clock, they looked at each other and decided they were not going to retire. But they were only taking local gigs on Friday and Saturday nights. Grant promised to get in touch with Herb and the rest of the employees. When he did, he found out the accounting department had put the paperwork in archives because they had a suspicion the Kentuckians would not retire completely. They made new corrections, advertisements went out in all the papers, and they were back in business. Some customers had to be rescheduled for later dates since they were doing only weekends. The crew was happy, the Kentuckians were happy, the crowds were happy, and most of all the girls were happy.

Chapter 12

Bella looked out the window of their upstairs bedroom. Hamilton land stretched as far as she could see. After all these years, she had to admit she loved it here. Her life had been good in so many ways. She loved her work with the business. Her home wasn't what she would have chosen, but it was comfortable. She had plenty of help in the kitchen, and housework would be provided when she wanted. The boys were grown men now, and she was proud of them. Jeremy was stationed at the Pentagon; she had no idea what he did. Jesse was home safe at the ranch. Good health had been with the family. Whit had never changed, but they had reached a plateau in their marriage. She had continued to love Grant, and he still loved her. He quit asking when she would be with him. By now, she knew she would not. Both wondered why they didn't put a stop to this.

More thoughts of the family drifted through her mind. Two years ago, Jeremy met Lillian at a coffee shop on the base. They ordered the same drink. They sat at a small table and found they liked many of the same things. Lillian worked on base in a civilian job, so she understood friendships could be fleeting. They spent as much time together as they could, never knowing when he would be deployed. It happened, so they got married by a chaplain on base. They had leave time before the new job, so they flew to Montana for his parents' blessing. They loved Lillian. She did make it clear she had no desire to live on a ranch! Jeremy did not plan on leaving the Marines soon. Jesse and Amy had been together for two years. They were students at MU. They wanted to get married but hadn't set a date. Amy, too, did not want to live on the ranch, but this was Jesse's job. She graduated with a degree in psychology and wanted to be a social worker. She was worried about work in a small town. They hadn't worked this problem out yet. Bells thought how much easier it was for her and Whit.

Clark had retired from the supermarket. The employees gave him a huge retirement party in the store. The store was closed for one evening. They decorated every aisle with streamers. The cafeteria tables had lighted candles. The bakery department baked a huge cake in the shape of the store, which was a work of art. Speeches were made and tears were shed. The proverbial gold watch was presented with fanfare. Clark and Meg were enjoying his retirement by traveling to the places they missed due to his work. They were well and happy.

Bella smiled as she thought about Nancy. She had made things stressful for Meg and Clark for a few years. She never got over the crush she had on Tom, Whit's attendant at the wedding. At first,

Tom had ignored her, but she kept chasing him. Tom asked Whit what he thought if he asked her out.

"What the hell are you talking about? She's just a stupid kid!"

"I know, but I thought if I took her out, she would say I'm an old cowboy set in his ways!"

"And if she doesn't? Then what?"

"I'll go back to ignoring her."

Tom asked Clark if he could take her on a date.

"No! You're too old!"

"Oh, let her go, Clark! She's had a crush on him all these years. He won't hurt her. If he did, Whit would kill him."

"I guess you're right! One date."

One date continued for several months. In March of her senior year of high school, she got pregnant. The Archer household was in a frenzy. They finally decided not to do anything for the 3 months of high school. Nancy was thrilled and Tom found he was excited about the baby. They got married the Sunday after graduation. He took her to the ranch, and she loved it! They made a spare bedroom into a nursery. He bought everything imaginable for a new baby. He let her buy whatever furnishings she wanted for the house. Tom had never been happier. Their little boy was born before Christmas. They loved him and named him Thomas Clark. They didn't care who counted on their fingers from their wedding day to the birth of Thomas.

Chapter 13

One morning, Whit and Jesse saddled Blue and Queen and rode out to one of the four corners of the ranch to check it out. The wranglers did a fine job, but they liked to go for themselves. Father and son were enjoying the ride. They saw two eagles circling around their aerie. They didn't ride close, so they weren't sure if there were babies. Hawks were sitting on fence posts hoping for a rodent or a rabbit for lunch. Jack rabbits ran in front of the horses, avoiding the hawk. Meadowlarks were sitting on the barbed wire busily chirping. A few stray cattle were huddled in a group. They rode over to check them out. The cattle moved away not wanting to be disturbed. A rattlesnake scurried along the ground. Jesse drew his gun and shot him. "Good aim!" Whit praised. They did not belong to the "bleeding hearts" that said snakes keep rodent population down. They hated rattlesnakes; they bit cattle and horses, and people, if someone was careless.

They turned around and leisurely started back. Father and son had a long visit during the ride, solving small problems and sharing funny stories from the cowboys. They were almost home when Whit stopped Blue and dismounted. Jesse reined up Queen.

"What's going on, Dad?" he asked, concerned. Whit took off his hat and put his head on Blue's neck and held onto his mane with his hand.

"I've got one hell of a headache. It just came as we started back. Never had anything like it."

"I don't know what to do, Dad! Want me to call Mom? I think we have cell."

"No, just give me a minute." He closed his eyes for a bit. He slowly mounted Blue, and they walked the horses back to the house.

"I'll take care of the horses. You get in to see mom." He was worried.

Whit entered the kitchen and sat down. "Bella!" He threw his hat on the counter. He still had his gun belt on. Bella came into the kitchen.

"Whit! What in the world is going on?" She stood beside him, concerned.

"I got one hell of a headache coming back. I got off Blue and put my head on his neck hoping the warmth would help, but it didn't."

"I'll get some Tylenol." He gulped them and continued to sit quietly.

"Want to go to the emergency room?"

"No. I'll go lie down on the couch for a while." He dropped his gun belt on the floor, stepped over it and went into the living room to lie down. Bella picked up his hat and gun belt and put them away in the mud room, then went to check on him. He had fallen asleep. She stared at his face, wondering if he had had a stroke or heart attack. He didn't look like that had happened. Jesse came in.

"How is he?" He was becoming more afraid.

"I gave him some Tylenol. He seems to be sleeping OK."

"What do you think? Shall we call an ambulance?"

"He said no. Let's see how he does tonight."

Jesse thought they should call the ambulance, but he went along with his mother. Whit woke up and said he was hungry. He said the pain was better. He ate something, then went to bed. The next morning, he thought he was fine. Bella still tried to talk him into going to the emergency room, but he still refused.

"I'm going to the barn to see what Jesse is doing," he informed Bella. She pleaded with him to wait a while, but he said no. She watched him struggling to make it to the barn, then he disappeared into the corral. He turned around to hook the gate and collapsed to the ground landing on his face.

Bella had called Jesse in the barn to watch for Whit. Jese came out and saw his father on the ground.

"Dad!" He screamed and rushed to Whit. He turned him on his back and saw he was unconscious. He ran into the tack shop and grabbed two horse blankets. He put one under Whit's head and covered him with the other. He dialed 911 on his cell phone.

"Carol, this is Jesse Hamilton. Dad has collapsed in the corral and he's unconscious. Send the ambulance!"

"Right away, Jesse." They were on the way. He called his mother.

"Mom, Dad collapsed in the corral. I've called 911 and they'll be here soon!"

"Oh! I'll be right there!"

The ambulance arrived the same time Bella entered the corral. She watched the paramedics put him on a stretcher and into the ambulance. He still was unconscious. They gave him oxygen.

"Do you want to ride with us, Mrs. Hamilton?" They offered kindly.

"Uh, no. I will drive in." They looked at her, surprised.

" I will!" Jesse stated, and jumped in. The ambulance took off with siren blaring. She watched until it vanished. 'I want to call Grant.'

Several cowboys met her as she returned to the house.

"Mrs. Hamilton! What happened? Is he going to be ok?" She didn't want to give out any information until later. Eddie came up.

"Bella, what's going on? What can I do to help?" He was the only person that called her by her first name.

"I don't know anything yet. Jesse rode with him in the ambulance. I want you to be in charge until he gets back. Make sure things go on as usual."

"Yes, of course. Ok, guys let's go back to work. Mrs. Hamilton will let us know when there is a definite diagnosis."

"Thanks, Eddie," she said and went into the house. She stopped in the kitchen to tell Maria that Whit was in the hospital. "Please make sure there is food, sandwiches, cookies, things like that in case people arrive." "Yes ma'am," Maria promised.

The most important calls to make were to the family. She went into Whit's office to call Sam and Edna.

"Edna, is Sam there? Whit collapsed in the corral and is unconscious. The ambulance came for him, and Jesse rode with them. I will be going soon after I call everyone."

"Oh my God, no! Not our precious Whit! Sam! Sam! We've got to go to the hospital! Whit's hurt!" She hung up before Bella could say anything. The phone rang. It was Tammy.

"Tammy, do you know anything? Were you there when he came in?"

"Yes, but my shift just ended. I don't think they know anything yet. Shall I come out to the ranch?"

"No, I've got a lot of calls to make, then I need to go to the hospital."

"Are you going to call Grant?"

"No, not until I know for sure what's wrong. Thanks, Tammy! Love, you!" She hung up. Next were her parents. Meg answered. Bella filled them in on what she knew and said she was leaving for the hospital. Meg said she would tell Nancy and Tom and they could help spread the word. She went upstairs to get ready to go to the hospital. While driving, she realized she hadn't had breakfast. She drove through a McDonald's and bought a breakfast sandwich and a large coffee. 'How can I possibly do this with my husband lying unconscious?' She finished her sandwich as she parked at the hospital. She threw the wrapper on the floor and sipped more of her coffee before she went in.

Whit was whisked into the emergency room and transferred to the table. There was no sign of response from him. They immediately hooked him up to monitors, drew vials of blood and did a portable chest x-ray. He was not improving. He was rolled into x-ray for a brain scan. It was not finished before they had a diagnosis. Whit had an aggressive glioblastoma that was progressing rapidly. The oncologist said there was nothing to do but make him comfortable. The neurologist and radiologist concurred.

They were stunned. They knew who he was, not personally, but knew of the Hamilton Ranch. To have this happen to such a young man was devastating to them, not to mention Whit's family. He was transferred to the ICU to monitor his regression. They debated on which one to tell the family. The ER physician said the son, Jesse, rode with the ambulance, but they had no idea where his wife was. They decided all of them would come to the reception area.

Sam and Edna arrived and were talking with Jesse, wanting to know what was going on. Jesse had been by himself with no sign of his mother. Bella walked in to three frightened people.

"Where have you been?" All accused her together.

"I notified people!" She belligerently retorted and glared at them.

"That could wait! Why weren't you here with your husband?" Sam moved toward her with Edna behind.

"I called you first!" Bella stood her ground and did not back off.

"I'm sorry, Bella," Sam apologized. "Yes, you did." He admitted humbly.

Other people were enjoying this Hamilton family argument. The doctors came in and noticed people staring.

"Let's go into the chapel," the ER doctor suggested. People settled back into their chairs. They were going to miss the good part.

They sat in the small chapel's pews. The oncologist cleared his throat and looked at each one.

"We have come to a diagnosis. The brain scan told us exactly what is wrong with Whit. He has a very serious brain tumor that is quickly growing. There is nothing we can do but keep him comfortable." He looked at the other doctors for support. Before they could offer their support, Sam stood up. "I am not going to take your diagnosis from a bunch of local yokel doctors! I will have him flown to the best cancer institute in the United States!" He bellowed. They stared at him.

"Sam, stop it!" cried Edna.

"Mr. Hamilton, do what you must, but by the time you get everything done, Whit will be gone. Try and brace yourselves for what is to come." The oncologist tried to be comforting and the other doctors shook their heads in agreement.

Jesse, Sam and Edna began sobbing. Bella took Jesse in her arms. "Jesse, we will work this out. I haven't reached Jeremy, but I'm sure he will be here as soon as he can get leave." She put her arms around Sam and Edna. In their sorrow, they did not notice she was not crying. She looked at the doctors. "Thank you for explaining this to us. We will get together as a family for comfort. May I see my husband now?"

"Yes, of course, Mrs. Hamilton. Let me take you to him. Just one at a time, please." The ER doctor took her to the ICU.

He opened the door for her. She walked to Whit's bed. She thought how this could be Whit. This small man hooked up to all these machines that were not going to save him anyway. He was as white as the sheet he was lying on. His hair still had dirt in it and was dull, like old straw. His arms had needles sticking in them with tubes running to IV bottles. An oxygen cannula was in his nostrils making it easier for him to breathe. She looked down at him.

"I don't know what to say, Whit. I can't imagine you like this. I guess it wouldn't have mattered if we had come in last night. I hope I can get through all this, and you would be proud of me." She turned around and left.

She entered the waiting room. "I am going to go home now. Jesse, can you ride with your grandparents? Perhaps you can drive. Sam and Edna, if you want, come in for a while. There is lunch and coffee." Jesse agreed. His grandparents were still in a state of shock. "Grandad, take Grandma in to see Dad. I'm sure they will let both of you in. I will wait here until you come back, then I'll go in to see him." There was still no answer, but Sam was able to help Edna stand and walk into Whit's room. They looked at their beautiful son they loved more than life itself. "Whit, we tried to do what we thought was right. You did perfectly! You took care of your wife and sons and increased our empire. Rest in peace, Son." Edna bent over Whit and kissed his pale cold cheek. She continued to sob. Sam led her back to the waiting room. Jesse looked at them, then entered his father's room. Looking at the shell of the man he was now, Jesse remembered yesterday how they were riding their beloved horses and having a glorious time. He leaned over and his tears ran down on Whit's chest. "Dad, how can I run the ranch without you? I don't know where to begin." He felt like he could hear Whit tell him he will do fine. He quit crying. He retrieved his grandparents and put them in the back seat of their car. Sam took Edna in his arms. They rode like that back to the ranch.

A few people had arrived: Meg and Clarke, Nancy and Tom, Greg and Tiffany, and Tammy and Jeff. Lunch had been served in the kitchen, but no one ate. Nothing was settled, so no plans could be made. Finally, they began to leave, and Bella was glad. She was exhausted. Jesse took his grandparents' home, then came back. Jesse checked with Eddie; everything was under control. "Thanks, Eddie. We will talk tomorrow." Jesse saw the house was quiet; Bella had gone to bed. He did the same.

A small, slim woman dressed in hospital scrubs was standing by Whit's bed. She had flaxen hair slipping out from her hospital bandana. She did not touch him. She bent over and held on to the bed rail.

"I am sorry, darling Whit. I am so sorry."

She turned to go. The hospital ID card clipped to the lanyard around her neck read, 'Frankie Pederson, Radiology.' The ICU nurse came in.

"Hi, Frankie! Checking on your patient?"

"Yes," she murmured.

"This is such a shame. Can't help but feel bad," she sympathized. Frankie nodded and slipped out the door.

The next day hadn't dawned yet. Soft light was in the eastern sky. Whit's eyes opened slightly. "Bella," he said, then closed his eyes permanently.

Dr. Pierce, the oncologist, called Bella.

"Mrs. Hamilton, this is Dr. Pierce. Mr. Hamilton passed away a little while ago. He was not in any discomfort and passed away peacefully." Bella thought his words sounded like an obituary.

"Thank you for calling." Silence.

"Mrs. Hamilton, is there anything I can do for you? Do you have any questions?"

"No. I need to call my family."

"Very well, then. I am sorry for your loss." 'What's going on with her? Well, everyone is different.' He started his morning rounds.

Bella had just woken up and was sitting on the edge of the bed when Dr. Pierce called. She rubbed her eyes and face. She rubbed her hands together and stood up. She felt dizzy for a moment. Slowly she went to the bathroom to get ready to face the long day ahead. She went downstairs and found Jesse was already outside.

"Good morning, Mrs. Hamilton," Maria greeted her. "I have coffee and breakfast. Would you like something"

"No, just coffee. Mr. Hamilton died this morning," she stated matter-of-factly. Maria gasped. "Oh, no!"

"Maria, it's OK. Did Jesse say where he was going?" Before Maria could answer, he came into the kitchen.

"Jesse. Dad died this morning. He never woke up."

"No! Oh, mom, I can't bear it! What will we do?"

"Jesse, it's all right. We will get through this. I need to call Jeremy and everybody else."

"Mom, let me call some."

"OK. I'll call both grandparents. You sure you can do it? Everyone may as well come here today so we can make arrangements." Jesse and Maria looked at each other, wondering how Bella could be so strong.

Bella took her coffee and went into Whit's office to make the calls. The first one will be the hardest.

"Hi, Edna. Is Sam with you?"

"Why, is he dead?"

"Yes, Edna, he is, early this morning. He never woke up. You and Sam come over later today so we can make arrangements." She could hear Edna screaming for Sam. He came to the phone. Bella repeated her message and told him to come over later. Sam hung up without a word.

"Mom, is dad with you?"

"Yes. Do you have bad news?"

"I do."

She managed to reach Jeremy on the first call. He was able to get an emergency time off for a week. Lillian did not wish to come.

By afternoon, everyone that loved Whit was there. They wanted to have the service in the high school auditorium as the church and funeral home could not seat all the people that would be there. The service wouldn't be for a week as there were so many cattlemen friends from other states would want to attend. Announcements were placed in local papers and Missoula, plus cattle-selling journals. A lunch with a probable open bar would be held at the country club. Bella did not want an open casket, but Edna and Sam insisted upon it. They compromised by having a viewing before the service and a closed casket during the service. 600 people attended, cattlemen from several states, horse breeders, and equipment company owners were there. Bella, Jesse, Jeremy and Sam stood in four different receiving lines to make sure everyone was greeted. This was too much for Edna. Meg and Clark took her back to her home where her personal maid cared for her. Bella thought the day would never end, but finally she, Jesse and Jeremy were back at the ranch. They were too exhausted to discuss the day's events and retired to their rooms.

Todd Hollingsworth wanted to have the reading of the will while Jeremy was still home. Everyone had copies of the will and knew how Whit's estate was divided. There would be no squabbling. The night before the reading, Edna, who had been recuperating, called Bella asking if she knew how to get into the safe where her copy was. Bella hadn't given it much thought. Yes, she knew where it was, and planned to get it out tonight. She hung up and found Whit's ring of keys. She needed one that would open the drawer that had the combination to the safe. He always kept it locked. She tried several with no luck and was getting exasperated. She went to the kitchen to get a soda. She went back with the soda, sipping as she went. She picked up the next key and continued until she found the right one.

She opened the drawer and looked at its sparce contents. A small revolver surprised her, but knowing Whit, it seems logical. She gently laid it on the desk. Small trinkets cluttered the drawer. She had no idea what they were. She picked up a little velvet ring box and opened it. There was a folded piece of paper with numbers. "Aha! I bet this is it!" She went to the wall safe and tried the combination several times before it snapped open. She thought there would be just one document, but there were three. She picked them up and carried them to the desk. One said, 'Settlement', next was 'Whit,' and third said, 'Last will and testament of Whit Hamilton.' She knew what that one contained, so she picked up 'Settlement.' She sat upright in her chair after she finished reading, then read it again. 'Whit got a 17-year-old girl pregnant. I never knew that' she mused. She read it one more time, then remembered a dirty old man and skinny teenager came to see Sam. They went into his office. They came out and the man gave her his name and phone number and spelled his name, Knosh, several times. Sam came out of his office agitated and told her to go home. So that's what the old man and girl wanted, hush money! But she also had an abortion. She put the document back in its folder and opened the document titled, 'Whit.'

Her life changed completely after reading this document. She reread it several times. By now, her hands were shaking, and tears blocked her reading. 'He never loved me. All this time, he never loved me. Our marriage was a farce and a terrible joke. How could his parents do that to him, and me?' She continued feeling furious. She would not mention this to her sons unless the need to tell them arose. She put that document back in the envelope and returned two of them to the safe, locked it, returned the gun back into the drawer and locked it. She swallowed the last of her warm soda.

Edna hung up the phone and sat down. Suddenly, she jumped up and cried:

"Sam! Oh my God! We must get over to the ranch before Bella opens the safe! I had forgotten those other two documents were stored in there!"

"God! How could we have made such a mistake? Why didn't we bring them over to our safe? Bella will be devastated if she reads them. Let's go!" They hurried to their car as fast as possible, drowning with guilt.

They walked into Whit's office and saw they were too late. Bella was still sitting in the chair with a dazed look. They ran to her, planning on engulfing her in their arms. Instead, she rose quickly. The chair rolled back until it hit the wall.

"Do not touch me!" she threatened. "How in the hell could you do that to your son? Just because he got that girl pregnant! You ruined his life! He was not in love with me! How could you do that to me, to all of us? Our marriage was a lie, even your grandsons are a lie! Those precious sons of mine and Whit's! None of us deserved this!" Her voice shook with rage. She never dreamed she could talk to Sam and Edna like this, but they deserved it.

Sam and Edna clutched each other. They deserved everything Bella threw at them.

"Whu, what are you going to do with this information?" stuttered Sam.

"Nothing right now, Sam. But I am saving it for a time if I should need it. Now, even though the will hasn't been read, we know this is now my house. So, get out!" She walked toward them.

"Jesse and I will pick you up in the morning to go to the reading. Jesse will know nothing of this."

They turned, still clinging to each other and left. She was right. This is her house now.

Jesse and Jeremy came home, laughing and swatting at each other like they did when they were kids. Bella could tell they had been drinking, but it was Jeremy's last night home.

"Hi, Mom! What're you doing still up?" they slurred.

"Waiting for you, just like I used to!" she retorted. They had no clue about the turmoil that had just ensued. "Now get to bed! We have a big day tomorrow."

They came to her and gave her slobbery kisses on her cheeks and jostled each other going up the stairs, again, just like when they were little.

She sighed, turned the light off, and went upstairs.

The next morning, they picked up Sam and Edna with the large van that had an extra seat in the back. Bella sat there, Sam and Edna in the back seat, Jeremy riding while Jesse drove. They were lost in their own thoughts.

Todd Hollingsworth ushered them into the same conference room used to change Whit's life so many years ago. Todd ordered coffee then closed the door.

"Good morning," he began. "We are here to finalize the last will and testament of Whit Hamilton." Edna sniveled. "I see you have your documents. There has been no change in the will since Whit's declaration several years ago. Bella is to inherit all his possessions to use as she feels fit. She inherits 50% of the business, Sam and Edna, 25% and Jesse and Jeremy 12 ½%. Anyone can sell their portion if they desire. Does anyone protest this?" he finished. No one spoke. Todd was expecting some backlash since this was written so long ago when no one was thinking about Whit's early demise. Finally, he said. "That is all I have at this time. The meeting is concluded." They rose, each shook his hand and said thank you, and left. It ended so fast that coffee was never brought in.

"I think we need to get something to eat before we take Jeremy to the airport," Jesse suggested. "Yes, I think we need sustenance after that," Bella agreed. They stopped at the restaurant where Tammy and Bella had lunch after the concert. She wanted to protest but realized that would be silly and they would ask why. They were seated on the other side of the room. She kept gazing over where they sat so long ago. She could hear Grant's every word and how he looked that night. "Mom, what are you looking at, do you see someone you know?" Jesse asked. 'Yes, I do, I see someone I love very much.' "Just looking to see if there is any artwork on that side of the room," she lied. Food helped the atmosphere and they visited quietly until it was time to go to the airport.

A parking place was available close to the airport entrance. They got out of the car to wish Jeremy a safe journey home. He hugged his grieving grandparents and wondered if he would ever see them again. Edna and Sam kissed him on both cheeks at the same time. "Sure, hope you don't have to go overseas," Sam said. "Don't worry Grandad, I'll be fine no matter what," he assured him. Jesse shook his hand and said nothing. He was choked up and didn't want it to show. Jeremy knew, he felt the same. He took his mother in his arms. "Mom, I love you so much! I wish dad hadn't left us." "We'll do fine, Jeremy. Don't worry, I promise," she comforted him. He took his duffel bag out of the trunk, swung it over his shoulder and confidently waved at them at the airport entrance. Jesse helped his grandparents get comfortable in the van while Bella sat in the front seat. Quiet conversation was held on the way home. Jesse helped his grandparents into their home. "I'm going to find Eddie to check on things and put the van away. We won't be needing it for a while." Bella entered the quiet house and went upstairs. She sat on her bed and burst into tears. These were the only tears she shed. 'This was bound to catch up with me,' she reasoned. She rolled over on her stomach across the bed and cried until she was exhausted. A warm bath felt good. Leisurely soaking in the fragrant bath salts, she composed herself, dried off and went to bed. She felt much better the next morning.

Chapter 14

She was sitting in Whit's office talking to Tammy. She had told her everything. Tammy was stunned about what Whit's parents had done to him. She consoled her friend as best she could. Bella needed someone to talk to. Jesse came into the office with a frown on his face.

"I've got to go now. Jesse just came in looking upset. Thanks for being here for me."

"Of course, Love you, Bella."

"Love you too, Tammy. Thanks for being here."

"Son, what's wrong?"

"Mom, we need to decide what to do about some help for me. Like I said earlier, I want to have Eddie to help me. He has been with us since before I was born. He loves it here and I know you used to date him a long time ago. Can we put him on as assistant manager? Guess that would make me manager!" He laughed. "That sounds silly!"

"OK, if you think that's best. I agree with you, he has been loyal. Have him come in to fill out paperwork, then I'll send it to the accountant at Hollingsworth. You will be manager, then. May as well change that status too!"

"Do I get a raise?"

"Quit being silly!"

"Now, one other thing, I need someone under Eddie to help him. He can't handle it all yet. How about Gus Henry? He's been a straw boss for years. I know I'm throwing a lot at you, but I know Dad would want me to keep things running smoothly."

"OK, let's do it. See how it goes." How could she ever get away to see Grant? She sat staring out the window, discouraged.

The next morning, Sam called her.

"Bella, Edna and I want to set an appointment with you."

"Sam, you don't need an appointment. Come over now, if you wish."

"Be right there."

She rubbed the back of her neck. What in the world is the matter now? I hope they are alright. She watched them drive up. He helped Edna out of the car. It was sad to see how this vibrant woman and shrunken man could be the same couple a few weeks ago. They came into the office and sat down with no greeting.

"Good morning," opened Bella. They ignored it.

"We are moving to Arizona to a place called Paradise Valley, in north Phoenix." He took a breath.

"You are what?"

"You heard me. We are flying to Phoenix tomorrow and meeting a real estate lady to show us properties. Then we will be back to get ready to move. Don't interrupt me! I'm going to say this all-in-one piece! Now, we are giving the house to Jesse. We are having Hollingsworth draw up the papers for us to sign. We don't want a thing in there. We will buy all new things in Phoenix. I haven't told Jesse yet. We are hoping his girlfriend will consider living in town so they can get married. Edna and I want to sell our 25% to anyone, as soon as possible, we don't care who buys it. I never want to set foot on Hamilton Ranch property again. There is nothing here for us since our son is dead. Do I make myself clear to you, Bella?"

Bella would not give him the satisfaction of asking him to repeat what he said.

"Yes, perfectly clear. I wish you well." She stood up to usher them out. They were not expecting her to end the meeting. They gathered themselves together and slowly marched by her and left.

She was shaking so badly she could barely walk back to her chair. She held her hands together to keep them from trembling. She wondered if she should be glad or sad. She was both. She needed to tell Jesse and Jeremy, then Todd Hollingsworth, but most of all, she wanted to tell Grant.

Jesse was gone for the day. She put on a jacket from the mud room and walked to the mailbox, like she did years ago, hoping for a letter from Grant. How far she had come! Was it better, or worse? Todd called her later that afternoon. He said all the paperwork had been done; Jesse owned the house free and clear, and paperwork was signed saying Sam and Edna were selling their shares of the ranch. She was glad to hear from him, she felt more secure and in control. She sat at her desk until Jesse came home.

"Hi, Mom! I'm starving! Going to the kitchen to get something to eat!" he exclaimed jubilantly.

"No, I want you to come into the office. I have something to tell you."

"Can't it wait?"

"No. not this time." He sauntered into the office, teasing his mother.

"Ok. I had company this morning, Sam and Edna. They are moving to Phoenix. Here's more: they are giving you the house, free and clear, so you can marry Amy. Finally, they are selling their 25% portion of the ranch. Sam said he never wants to set foot on Hamilton land again." She studied Jesse's face. He reminded her of Whit when he was controlling himself before he spoke.

"Well, I'll be damned! We need to go over this again, but not right now. Honestly, Mom, I don't know what to think. I don't even know if Amy will live there. If I moved there, you would be all alone in this big house. I don't want to do that to you. Yes, lots of thinking is going to have to be done." He leaned against the desk, looking at his mother.

"You are right, Jesse. But I had to tell you right away. I don't think they will change their minds. They are flying to Phoenix tomorrow to meet with a realtor. I need to tell Jeremy, too, although it doesn't involve him so much. You may as well go eat. Nothing is going to change tonight." He stood up and went to the kitchen. Bella wondered if this was the time to tell him about Grant. Maybe they were over, they hadn't talked for weeks. He still doesn't know about Whit. No, the right time will come to tell the boys.

Sam and Edna boarded the plane in first class. They were breathless from the rushing and making sure they didn't forget anything. The flight attendant came to offer them drinks and breakfast. They were quiet until the food and coffee came. They enjoyed the continental breakfast, juice and coffee. The two-hour flight to Phoenix went quickly. A limousine chauffeur met them inside the airport and picked up their luggage, then led them to the limo and drove them to their luxurious resort Sam booked for a few days. They were used to fine hotel accommodation, but they did say this was lovely and they planned on enjoying their stay in Phoenix. They ate an early dinner, then strolled around the grounds enjoying the plants and bushes not seen in Montana.

Francine Olliver, the realtor, picked them up at 8 a.m. the next morning. She was tall and slim and dressed in a wine-colored summer suit with a very short skirt. Black high heels were on her capable feet. Brightly painted toes peeking out the open shoes. Her short blonde pixie haircut framed her heavily made-up face. Gold earrings, along with studs at the tops of her ears finished her outfit. She carried a laptop and cell phone. She was one of Pheonix's top realtors and had been featured in several real estate magazines. She knew how to show a home efficiently, leaving nothing of importance left out.

They waited for her in the lobby. She ushered them into her Bentley SUV and expertly drove in and out of the crowded streets. They arrived at the first mansion. They were impressed, but she showed them three more homes, then took them to lunch at a quiet bistro used exclusively for realtors trying to close a sale. After lunch, Francine asked them which one they decided.

, never offering them any more homes. She knew they would take one.

"We chose the first one," Sam told her. He expected her to gush and tell him they made an excellent choice. She did not. She knew they would take that one. She had begun the paperwork earlier.

"We will pay cash," he said. He thought she would be amazed. He did not know most of her sales were cash.

"Very well, Mr. Hamilton. Let's go to my office and finish," she cooed.

Sam and Edna were happy with their new home. Since they had a few days left, they wanted to look around the valley. He hired a limo for 2 days. The driver was a Phoenix native. He became a tour guide and showed things he thought they would enjoy. After the two days they had enough and were ready to go back to plan what they would need to bring to the "Valley of the Sun" for the rest of their lives. They looked forward to buying new furniture. They still had no intention of bringing any of their things to Phoenix. They did just that and began their new lives in Paradise Valley, never once looking back. All that was left was to sell their portion of the ranch.

Bella decided this was the day to call Grant. Jeremy could wait. Jesse went to work as usual. She sat in the bedroom and used the extension there. She dialed him on the house phone.

Grant was in his office paying his personal bills. He did not like doing them. Jake kept walking on his keyboard and jumping in his lap. He put Jake on the recliner with his favorite soft toy. Soon he cuddled up with it and went to sleep. His cell phone rang with a Montana number. He answered it.

"Grant! Oh, thank God you answered! I didn't know if you would."

"Bella, honey, how are you? We haven't talked for so long! Are you OK?"

"No, I'm not. Are you free to talk for a while?"

"Yes, for today. Home paying bills. Are you sick?"

"Not physically. Well, maybe a little. Grant, Whit is dead."

"What? You say he's dead? When?"

"Grant, I want to tell you the whole story."

She started with Whit's headache and ended with what Sam and Edna did yesterday. He didn't interrupt. He was too stunned to say anything but, "Uh huh" or, "Oh, my God." She came to the end, breathless.

"Bella, honey, I should have been there. Oh, of course not, but now I am. What are you going to do?"

"Grant, darling, I don't know, I only know I need you."

"You want to come here? You can stay as long as you want."

"That would be wonderful. There are too many things unsettled. Jesse has a lot to think about, he needs to know if Amy will live in this town. She is a social worker and wonders if there would be any clients here. Jesse has hired an assistant manager and straw bosses. We must see if they work out. That' s all I can think of right now. Can you come here? Guess this would be the time to tell my sons about us, if there still is an us."

"Bella, honey there always will be an us. Can I tell you what's going on here?"

"Yes, Grant. I will give you the consideration you gave to me."

"The main thing, we are done touring, but we decided to stay together for a while. We play on Friday and Saturday nights. That's kind of the gist of it for now."

"Maybe you could come for 4-5 days?"

"Let me see, I could maybe do that. Shall I call you on this number now?"

"Yes! I will cancel my cell phone, maybe smash it up, what do you think?" They chuckled. "Grant, please come so we can start our life together!"

"You haven't said how you feel about Whit dying, Bella."

"I don't know, I've been mostly numb. After what his parents did to him, and that he didn't love me, I think it was easier going on with my life with you."

"OK, honey, let me see what I can do, and we can decide what to do about telling everyone about us. Frankly, I want to start our life together. Give me a few days to sort this all out. I love you still, Bella."

"I love you, Grant! Call me soon."

They hung up and sat staring at nothing. Their lives were changing. Decisions needed to be made. Was it time to tell everyone? But first, they needed to spend time together with just them. It was exciting!

Grant understood why she couldn't come right now. The ranch was a huge operation and they had just lost the man who controlled it. Granted, Jesse was capable, but he was going to need good help he could rely on. Bella needed to be there to discuss progress in the new assistant manager and lesser bosses. Then there was the problem of Jesse moving out and possibly getting married. He thought seriously of going to Montana. He called Buzzy and asked him to come to the house. He had confided in Buzzy because he knew he could trust him.

"Hi, Grant; what's going on?"

"Buzzy, I need to tell you about a phone call from Montana." He told Buzzy his dilemma, should he even think about going for a few days?

"Grant, I think you should talk to Herb Ellers about the legality of the situation. Then talk to the boys and see if it's OK with them. The retirement thing might come up again. This is what I think." he delivered his honest opinion.

"That's along the line that I was thinking. I think I should see if Bella and I are happy together and what her sons think of me. Do you think I would stir up a lot of controversy? Do you think I would be in any danger? I know that sounds silly, but after we came home off the tour, I had to call the cops to help me get into the house."

"Those are serious concerns. Of course, you will stir things up, you are famous, and they probably don't have any celebrities living there. It might be a little hard on Bella's reputation to see she is hooking up with you. How soon do you want to go?"

"That's my main concern. I think I should wait a while. I'll get a better feeling for things when she calls. Thanks, Buzzy. You have been my rock all these years."

"Any time, Grant. Keep me posted."

Bella didn't call for two weeks. He was beside himself fretting.

"Grant, Jesse and Amy are going to get married in a couple of weeks. Do you think you can come?" He was so relieved he couldn't think of what to say. Then he knew he had to check with Herb and the band before he could commit to coming.

"Bella, I must talk to our band's lawyer for legalities. I know that seems weird, but since I am a celebrity, I must be careful. And I finally need to tell the boys what's been going on all these years and see if I can go between gigs. I will talk to them and get back in a few days. I hope it will be possible."

"I know. Those are things I need to learn to understand. Just need to be patient. We have been "patient" all these years! Let me know! I love you, Grant!"

"I'll get started right away. Bella, honey, one of these days it will be over."

He made an appointment with Herb in two days. He was nervous telling Herb all these things after keeping silent for so many years. Herb listened patiently until Grant was finished. He explained the legal issues to Grant and warned him not to do anything rash and to be careful, just like you would in a crowd. He didn't think he needed a bodyguard "since he wasn't a twenty-year-old rock star". They laughed, but if he felt uncomfortable, get one.

"Let me know what the band decides. I wish you the best of luck, Grant. You have been alone for so many years. You deserve some happiness."

Telling the band would be harder. They had a rehearsal the next Wednesday before Friday night's gig.

"Sit down, guys. I need to talk to you. I have put this off long enough. You need to know about Bella and me," he began. They looked at each other and thought it was about time he confessed. He told them the newest circumstances; that he wanted to go to Montana between gigs. They were silent because they didn't know what to say. Huey began.

"Grant, we are happy for you. Wish you would have shared this with us from the beginning! That was a lot of baggage to carry with you. So, what are your long-range plans?"

"I'm not sure. This is a lot for me right now. She can't come here. There is too much going on. This is a huge operation, not like 10 acres and two or three cows. I asked her to come here for a visit, but for now, it's out of the question. So, tell me honestly, do you think I can get away for a few days between weekends? Honest opinions, please." He looked at Rick, and Rick answered him.

"This is a lot, I agree. We can handle rehearsals because we don't need it anymore. Maybe if this works into something permanent, we might need to think about retiring. I hate to admit it, but sometimes I'm tired and don't want to go. Come on, guys, help me out here."

Grant was surprised. He looked around to see if the others agreed with Rick. No one jumped up and said, "Let's retire!" but no one disagreed with him. They continued discussing the pros and cons and decided to wish him well in Montana. They would go on from there when he got back. They were scared, even Grant, when the subject of retiring came up more than once.

Grant was relieved when Bella did not call back until after Jesse's and Amy's wedding, although he was a little hurt. But that made a few more weeks past Whit's death so when he did go, it wouldn't look so bad for Bella. He knew in his heart, it would, everyone loved Whit.

"Are you caught up enough that an old broken-down country singer can come and woo the beautiful widow?" he asked slyly.

She laughed with joy and said, "When are you coming?"

"I will get a round-trip ticket for next Sunday morning and return Friday morning for the gig that night. What do you think?"

She lost her voice for a moment. "It's happening! All these years! No more wishing and planning for disappointment. Now it will be happiness only. Are you as excited as I am?"

"I'm just as happy as you are. Will you come to Missoula to get me? And don't be afraid of the old guy in jeans and a sweatshirt and cap pulled down, OK? I could rent a car if you can't."

"Call me and I will be there. Will I have to fight the crowd around you?"

"I hope not. OK, girl, this is it! See you on Sunday, Bella."

"I know."

They sat quietly in their own homes, excited and nervous at the same time. Their love is finally being fulfilled.

Bella knew the time had come to tell the boys. First would be Jesse. She saw him come to work and hollered at him to come to the house.

"What's going on?"

"I need to tell you something. But first, do you remember the time you and Jeremy rode with Dad to buy cattle and he bought you BB guns?"

"Yes! That was a big deal. So, what about it?" he wondered.

"That night Tammy and I went to Missoula to see a country singer named Grant Bartlett. Have you heard of him?"

"Of course! He's great!"

"He's coming here this Sunday morning."

"What? Why?" He looked at her, curious.

"He is coming to see me."

"Then what?"

"I don't know," she answered honestly. "We are friends, have been since that night. We have been corresponding for years. Now he is coming to see me."

"Did Dad know?"

"No."

"Well, I guess you know what you are doing. I'm not sure I like it."

"I understand. We do care about each other. We want to see where this will go." She wished she hadn't said that. He shook his head and went back outside. What was his mother getting herself into messing around with him, he wondered.

She was happy Jesse knew but was worried about his attitude toward Grant when he got here. She texted Grant and told him what happened. He read her text and was relieved it went well, or so it sounded. He texted her back and said he would rent a car in Missoula and drive to the ranch. He thought he would enjoy driving. He would use his GPS in his phone to find the ranch. He anticipated that they could greet each other with hugs and kisses, things they could not do at the airport. Finally, they could begin what they had missed after all these years.

Chapter 15

Sunday morning was here at last! Bella was too nervous to eat but tried a fresh cinnamon roll and coffee. She choked on the roll, then spilled coffee on her clothes. When she got her breath, she screamed. Maria came running from the pantry.

"Oh, precious Jesus, are you alright, Miss Bella?" She saw the spilled coffee, wet clothes and tears running down her cheeks from choking.

"I'm fine," she muttered, hurriedly wiping her face and dabbing at her clothes she would have to change. "I am nervous waiting for our guest, Mr. Grant, to arrive. Be sure everything is fine like I asked," she said shakily.

"Sure, Miss Bella, everything will be perfect for your man friend," she assured Bella, wondering who this Mr. Grant was.

She ran upstairs to redo her outfit. It had taken her an hour to pick out her new clothes. She put on jeans and a tee shirt and was furious with herself. She looked beautiful in her frustration, but she didn't know it. She sat on the bed, wringing her hands, waiting for the time to pass until he arrived at the ranch.

Grant did not fare much better. He got home from the show at 3 a.m. and didn't try to go to bed. He sat up in the recliner petting Jake. Jake kept up a steady purr, comforting Grant. Buzzy came for him at 6 a.m. He went inside the airport with Grant, mainly to protect him, but for once, no one noticed him. Buzzy gave him a hug when the boarding call sounded. "Have a great time, Grant. You deserve it!" Grant settled down in first class and enjoyed the continental breakfast. In two hours, he was in Missoula, rented his car, and checked the GPS on his phone. He was on the way to Bella, happily singing one of his songs.

He drove under the huge 'Hamilton Ranch' sign. He wasn't sure where to go since there was no house; it was all buildings. He noticed how well-kept the grounds were. Two cowboys rode up on horses to greet him. Bella had appointed them to keep watch. They didn't know who was coming. He got out of the car. The guys looked at each other. "Oh my God! It's Grant Bartlett!" They dismounted and came to greet him.

"Hello, Mr. Bartlett! We didn't know you were coming! Wow, we love your music! We know all your songs!" Grant was used to this, he heard it hundreds of times. Today was special.

"Hi, boys! Glad to hear it! I am looking for the house. Mrs. Hamilton is expecting me."

"Yes, that's why we're here, to escort you!"

Grant got back in the car and followed them. He smiled as he could tell they were discussing him. For once, he thought it was nice. They rode down the shaded lane to the main house. Grant was amazed at the beauty of it and the neat grounds here too. He saw her standing by the gate. He felt his heart would break with love for this beautiful woman. He sat in the car for a moment. The cowboys tipped their hats and galloped away. Bella stood still for a moment also, then she ran to him as he got out of the car. They stood holding each other, then their hearts and mouths melted together as if they were one.

"You're here," she cried, tears in her eyes.

"Yes, I am." He whispered in her hair.

"Never to leave again," they wished.

They walked arm and arm up the path and entered the kitchen. Maria and the girls had heard by now who was coming. They stood behind the counter giggling.

"Maria, this is Mr. Bartlett. We will come later for a lunch." The girls continued to giggle. Bella looked at them sternly. Grant grinned, amused.

They went up the stairs. At the top, Grant stopped.

"Where should I put my bag?" he asked quietly.

"In my bedroom," she answered softly.

They entered and Bella locked the door. They looked at each other, then Bella led him to her bed.

"Bella, this is yours and Whit's bed, isn't it? Are you sure?"

"Of course. If it makes you feel better, I put new sheets on it." They laughed, stood by the bed, and fell into each other's arms. They unbuttoned, unsnapped, and unzipped. Their hands crossed every line that couldn't be crossed before. Everything was new. It was gentle and fun. They experimented with things they could think of, liked some, ruled out others. They fell asleep tangled in each other's arms and the new bedsheet.

In the morning, they took a shower together and found lovemaking in the shower was too much. "My knees are shot!" he lamented. This brought on laughter. They were starving. They came into the kitchen. The girls started giggling and Bella glared at them. They scurried to make breakfast.

"I thought I would show you the ranch. Are you interested?" She hoped.

"Yes, I would like to see it. Are there cattle around?"

"For a while. We bring them here for winter and feed them hay."

She drove Whit's pickup out of the garage. She could still smell him. She wondered if Grant could, too, but how would he know what Whit smelled like? 'I should have cleaned his truck.' His work-worn leather gloves and a couple of baseball caps were in the back seat. A rope and a cattle prod were under her seat. She could feel them on the backs of her legs. An open can of half-filled Pepsi was in the cup container.

"Was this Whit's truck? He was a working man. I admire that. Bella, you must admit what happened to him was sad," he mused.

She didn't want anything to spoil this happy time. She pulled up by a shed, got out, and tossed his things on the ground by the door. Tears blinded her.

"Bella, honey, stop it!" Grant got out to help her. "It's all right! He was your husband for a long time."

"I don't want him to spoil our day!"

"He's not going to! Come on, I want to see this ranch!"

She quieted as they roamed through the lovely countryside. She showed him the brook. She didn't show him the sandy beach. On the way back, they stopped to look at the horses. He wanted to stay and spend time with them. She said they could come on Wednesday and ride, if he wanted. He was excited about that.

It was late afternoon when they got back to the house. There was beef stew and corn bread for supper. Dessert was apple pie from their orchard. They went into the family room and sat together on the sofa talking about their day, leaving out her tantrum. The TV wasn't holding their interest, and they went upstairs. Any cares were forgotten as they laid on the new sheets. In the morning, they filled the hot tub with warm water and bubble bath. They could make love there easier than the shower.

Tuesday, she wanted to show the town to him. It was her whole life, never living anywhere else. She did not want to move. She hoped Grant would not insist she move to Nashville. But she was not going to let this interfere with these four days. She took the car this time. She showed the superstore where Clark worked after he came home from Viet Nam. She drove past the house where she grew up; She did not stop; her parents were coming to dinner tomorrow night. The same with Jesse's small mansion. Grant was amazed at how magnificent it was. He thought what a wonderful home for Amy and Jesse to build a life.

"Do you feel like going into a coffee shop?" She thought it would be fun to 'show him off,' even though she knew there would be gossip. He examined the area and decided to give it a try. They entered the town's usual watering hole. He thought better of it after they came in.

"Oh my God! It's that country singer, what's his name! Hamilton cowboys told us he was here." They swarmed on him before he sat down. Someone ran outside yelling, "Grant Bartlet's here! Come and see him!" Suddenly, there were 15 people shoving cell phone cameras in his face, wanting to take selfies with him. He gave Bella a sour look, then changed his persona and signed autographs and let the crowd take selfies until they were satisfied. He smiled and chatted with them, then said he had to leave. They got in the car. Bella said, "I'm sorry Grant! I've got to learn!" "It's OK, I'm used to it" They drove up to a kiosk and ordered two larger lattes. She took him to several small villages in the area, then arrived home. He loved the scenery and the comradery of the people even though they pestered him. That night in bed they discussed all aspects of the trip that day. They were happy with their adventure.

Grant still wanted to see the horses. Bella had Luke, one of the cowboys, to get two horses saddled and ready to ride. Grant was thrilled to see them and anxious to try his luck at being a cowboy. He didn't have experience with horses. He should have as he portrayed one with his songs. Bella knew the horses; one was her's, and the other one was Queen, Jesse's horse, who was used for pleasure riding. She asked Jesse if it would be OK if Grant could ride her. It was hard for him to say yes, but Bella said they would only be walking. Bella mounted her horse. Whit had turned her into an excellent rider. Luke held Queen and tried not to grin as he watched Grant trying to mount Queen. Finally, he went over to Grant and showed him how to put his foot in the stirrup and swing his leg over Queen's back. This caused a lot of grunting trying to pull himself into the saddle. Queen couldn't believe this guy had no idea what to do. She was getting tired of standing still and began walking. Grant panicked. Luke ran after Queen and pulled on her reins.

"Gosh, don't you know anything about riding a horse?" he asked Grant. Bella took over and he knew he had made a mistake. "Sorry, Mr. Bartlett," he apologized profusely. He gave him a quick lesson on how to hold the reins. Bella led them out of the corral and knew they would just be going on the road for a short ride. She tried to reassure him, but he was afraid he would do something wrong, and Queen would start running. Queen knew he was afraid. She walked along slowly. Bella ended the ride early. Luke helped Grant off Queen and caught him as his legs were weak. He hobbled to the car, never more embarrassed in his life. Bella told him it would be easier the next time. He soaked his body, by himself, in the hot tub and took a nap. Tonight was the big supper with the family.

Bella went upstairs to wake him. He was lounging in bed with his hands clasped behind his head. He grabbed her and pulled her on his stomach. She nuzzled his neck and thought about giving him a hickey.

"Stop it! Company will be coming soon!"

"OK," he said as he ran his fingers through her hair, messing it up.

"My jeans and a polo shirt and my cowboy boots, OK? My hats are in boxes in my closet in Nashville," he worried.

"That's fine. See you in a little bit." She scampered down the stairs.

He smiled as he got dressed. He went down the steps slowly as his thighs were sore from the horseback ride. He told himself to be careful so they wouldn't realize he was not a real cowboy.

Meg and Clark were their first guests. They felt a little shy, as did Grant. Soon, they were visiting and relaxed, possibly the beer helped. Nancy and Tom were next. Nancy tried not to stare but did anyway. Grant tried to make her feel better, telling her was just as regular guy. Tom shied away from him. He missed his good friend, Whit, and wondered how this new romance took place so fast. Grant knew what he was thinking. He did not push the friendship. Greg and Tiffany arrived shortly after Nancy and Tom. Grant felt the same way since Greg was Whit's best friend. Tiffany was smart and cute, and was used to attention, so she was not fascinated by a celebrity. Jesse and Amy came in; Jesse was anxious to meet Grant to see if he could decide what his mother saw in him. Grant did his best to make Jesse understand how close his mother and he were. Jesse found it hard to warm up to Grant. Amy ignored him. He felt like she probably did that to a lot of people. He did not care for her and made no attempt to get on her good side. Last to arrive were Tammy and Jeff. She had to complete her shift in the ER.

"Mr. Bartlett! So, we meet again! This is great and you have made Bella so happy all these years!" she babbled. The conversation stopped. They looked at her questioningly. Bella wanted to strangle her.

"Well, little lady, I see you haven't changed much after all these years! You talk just a little too much!" Grant put her in her place, but the damage had been done.

"Come on, Tammy, let's get a drink," Jeff coaxed. He was angry with her, too, and gave Bella an apologetic look.

The conversation started up again and was forgotten. Fantastic barbecued ribs, cowboy beans and coleslaw with fresh baked bread and mounds of butter were served by the experienced help. They knew they were appreciated. Thanks were said many times during the conversation. Apple pie was served later with whipped cream or ice cream. Lights and heaters were set up on the patio. A brandy or bourbon bar was tended by one of the cowboys who played bartender. People finally began to leave, knowing Bella and Grant had only one day left before he left Friday morning.

Both were exhausted as they slowly climbed the stairs. They were happy that he met all the family and friends. They saved the discussion for the next day, and, for one night, went to sleep immediately.

Jesse woke them up at 7 a.m. the next morning.

"Mom! Can you come down here? Need to talk to you!" he yelled urgently.

"What happened?" Grant asked sleepily.

"I don't know. It is serious or he would not have yelled at me. She rolled over and put on her robe and slippers and hurried down to meet him.

"Mom, two calves have runny noses. Charley is here examining them right now. I sent Eddie out with a couple of guys to look for ragweed, or something."

"OK, let's see what Charley thinks. I'll get dressed and be right out. You have them in the barn, don't you?"

"Yes. Sorry about interrupting your sleep."

"You know that's OK. See you in a bit," she called as she hurried up the stairs.

"Grant, I'm so sorry, but this is important, and I have to go," she stated.

"Of course, I understand. I'll get dressed and come to the barn. Is that OK?"

"Yes, that's fine. I want you to see what's going on," she answered as she threw on jeans and a sweatshirt. She picked up her work boots in the mud room and entered the stall in the barn.

"OK, Charley, what's the verdict?" she asked, worried. Charley was the veterinarian for Hamilton Ranch before she married Whit. He stood up. He had finished drawing blood from each calf and giving antibiotic shots.

"They don't seem sick; they are eating and drinking. There is no diarrhea or fever. I'm hoping they just got into something." He rubbed the calves' necks as he spoke. "I've already sent Bud with the blood vials to Missoula. Checking for infections like pneumonia. We should have the results by noon or one. I'm not too worried yet. They aren't coughing or sneezing, just snorting a little. I have another call. But call me if there are any changes. I'll bring the report to you as soon as it comes. Always glad to see you, Bella. Hear that country singer came to see you!"

"How did you hear that?" she asked, curious.

"Why, everybody knows he's here!" he replied with a grin.

"Here he is now, you may as well meet him. Charley, this is Grant Bartlett, the 'country singer!' Grant. Charley."

"Nice to meet you," they said together.

"I saw you when you were here many years ago. Great show!" Grant and Bella exchanged a quick look. Charley didn't notice as he entered his vet truck and drove away.

"What's wrong with the calves?" Grant looked at them with an inexperienced eye. He rubbed their soft ears between his fingers.

"Grant, it's like this. They have snotty noses, which could be pneumonia, or other serious things. Maybe they got into something in the pasture. That's what we are hoping for. I won't rest until we get the blood work back. Calves are our main source of income,

Grant. We raise them and sell them to feeders all over the United States. Some go to local feedlots that fatten them and sell to local slaughterhouses. If we lose a calf, we lose profit. But we care about them all. Whit and Sam loved them, and it always made them sad when they sold. But of course, they never could show that. Jesse is the same. I learned to feel that way, too. We also buy high quality heifers and save some of the babies for ourselves. We have a few high-quality bulls and do artificial insemination when needed. Charley does that for us. Grant, I love you so much! I know we didn't get time to think about our futures, but at least you can see I can't leave the ranch." She looked at him and wondered if this was goodbye.

Grant looked around her domain, saw the beauty of it, the responsibility, and her love for it all. He didn't say anything. His eyes went back to her, and he wanted to take her in his arms, but there were cowboys continually in and out of the barn, worried about the calves.

"Bella, honey, I will never ask you to leave this place. I understand your love for it and the animals that graze here. We will work it out, but not today. There are other things to worry about today. I love you too, Bella, honey, I love you, too."

They could not look away from each other. Later that night they would iron out a few of the problems facing them. Right now, the calves took priority. They went to the house for lunch, but Bella was too nervous to eat. Jesse stayed with the calves. They took lunch to him. Charley didn't make it there till 1 p.m. There was no pneumonia or infection. The calves were not snorting, so they left them in the corral for the night. Jesse stayed there in a small bunk room set up for such occasions.

They spent the rest of the afternoon and night together. The cook on duty that day grilled huge rib steaks. He added potatoes and asparagus to the grille. He served them quietly in the kitchen. They sat together on the bench, drinking red wine. He left them alone to fend for themselves.

Grant filled the hot tub and Bella added a fragrant bubble bath. They took the wine bottle with them and drank it until it was gone. They never got around to making plans, but it didn't matter. They knew he would be back.

He had to leave at 4:30 a.m.to arrive for 6 a.m. boarding to leave for Nashville. Grant backed the car and turned towards the road. He saw her standing in the same place she stood when he arrived. They waved and he drove down the tree-lined driveway.

Chapter 16

Buzzy met Grant at the airport. He called airport security and local police and told them Grant was returning. Grant would be dressed in old clothes, so probably there would be no problem, but just in case there was. Ben, a security guard, stood talking to Buzzy while watching the plane land. They became attentive as they studied the people leaving the plane.

"There he is!" Buzzy announced. Indeed, Grant wore jeans, a sweatshirt, and a baseball cap pulled down over his eyes. No one bothered him. Ben walked them to Buzzy's car. "Nice to see you back, Mr. Bartlett," Ben greeted him. "Thanks. And thanks for staying with Buzzy," Grant reciprocated. They got in the car and drove out of the airport.

"Well, how did it go?" Buzzy was anxious to hear.

"Buzzy, it was great! We were very happy. I am ready to go back. I will call a meeting on Tuesday with the band. I'm hoping we can decide on something permanent. Just keep this to yourself, Buzzy, like you have always done."

"That sounds serious, Grant. I think I agree with you. The guys don't say anything, but they seem to be tired after the shows and just go home. Maybe it is time to stop when we are ahead."

"Sounds encouraging! Those are my thoughts exactly!"

"I'll pick you up and take you to the bus tonight. You rest as long as you can," Buzzy offered.

"I'll take you up on that. Thanks."

Tillie and Jake were waiting at the kitchen door. He sat down on a chair as Jake made a wild jump into his lap and made biscuits. He stroked Jake's soft fur as Jake purred.

"Glad you are home, Mr. Grant! You want something to eat?" she asked.

"Glad to be here, too, Tillie. No, nothing to eat. I'm going to take a nap before the show tonight. We'll talk tomorrow. Thanks for being here." He took his flight bag and went to the bedroom with Jaske in toll. He fell on the bed and went to sleep. He managed to get ready before Buzzy came.

The guys were glad to see him but could tell he was in no condition to discuss his trip.

"Rick, you take a couple of sets tonight. Do you want to play lead, if not, that's OK. We can both play rhythm."

"Sure, Grant. That's fine with me. Hope the crowd doesn't complain."

"They'll probably be too drunk to notice." They were surprised at Grant's remark. He never criticized a crowd. He was always grateful for the fans. They looked at each other and wondered what happened on the trip.

"Monday we won't get together. I want to have a meeting with just you guys. If we come to a decision together, I will set up an appointment with Herb." Now they knew for sure something was in the works. In a way, they were hoping for good news. They had been talking among themselves during the days Grant was gone. Buzzy was right about his observation.

The show went on as usual. Grant was a true entertainer. The crowd never noticed how tired he was. They enjoyed Rick's adaptation of the songs. The band fell asleep as soon as the bus left for Nashville. They would be happy when tomorrow's show was finished. Buzzy took Grant home. Talking would wait until Tuesday. Saturday's show went fine, Rick took 3 sets this time. They had feelings the Kentuckians were coming to an end.

Grant slept all day Sunday and most of Monday. He and Bella talked between his naps. He told her he was having the meeting with the band on Tuesday. He was anxious to hear what they had to say about retiring. He thought he sensed a feeling of relief when he told them about the meeting. He asked about the calves. Bella said they were fine. She hired a spraying company to consult with her and Jesse. They said the ranch looked good, but they would do a few spots. She was pleased that Grant showed interest in the ranch.

Tuesday morning the Kentuckians had their meeting at the studio. Grant ordered a continental breakfast delivered. After their meal, Grant began his message.

"OK, boys, I had a great time in Montana. It is so great that I want to continue going there. I want to spend the rest of my life with this woman I have loved from afar for all these years. I do not want to entertain any more. So now is the time for you to say your part." His eyes roamed over the group and stopped at Rick. Rick cleared his throat and stood up.

"Well, Grant, I have been with you from the start. We made a ton of money together, and with these other guys." He looked at them. They nodded in agreement. "There is no reason why we wouldn't have a lot of money in our retirements. Maybe some residuals from records. We can get our social security soon. I am tired of entertaining. I am tired of the screaming and stomping, and the fans grabbing at us, or some wanting more. My stomach hurts more than it used to. Gracey and I have had our struggles through the years, but we've managed to stay together. Now she wants to go to some of the places we have been. She wants to be pampered at a nice resort. The kids are in college and don't need or want us anymore. It's time to quit, at least for me." He sat down. The studio was quiet.

Huey stood up. "I am the newest member of the group. I am just a kid," they laughed, "and I am ready to retire too. Everything Rick said is true. Rather than my stomach, my feet hurt so damned bad in those boots, and they are so hard to get off because my feet are swollen. I am getting high blood pressure and will have to go on medication soon. This means the world to me, but I want to leave while we are on top." He sat down.

The other stories were the same. Steve added that Chrissy had been diagnosed with breast cancer and he wanted to be with her for the struggle ahead. This was the first time they knew of Chrissy's cancer. Grant went to him and put his hand on Steve's shoulder. "God, Steve! If there is anything you need, let us know." He looked up at Grant and said," Let me go."

"For me, my eardrums are shot, I wonder why," Huey grinned. This broke up the sadness and they laughed with him. "We understand! We have had to listen to you behind us all these years!" Again, more laughter.

"I will call Herb and get an appointment before Friday's show. Be thinking about when to end them. How many more are booked?" They thought it was until just before Christmas. Grant said, "We should honor them, but no more!" "Amen!" they agreed. They departed in a jovial mood and hurried home to their families. Grant felt some 'buyer's remorse,' and hoped he did the right thing. He need not have worried. There was a celebration in each home, even Steve and Chrissy were happy and relieved.

Grant called Herb when he got home. The meeting was scheduled for Thursday afternoon. Herb had been expecting his call for the last several months. When the contracts were first drawn up a few years ago, he told the staff to put the paperwork in archives because he was sure they would not be retiring. Now, he told them to pull them back up and make copies of each one and put it into a folder so if there were changes, they could add or change before the final draft was printed for their signatures.

The guys sat down. Herb distributed each folder.

"Go over each item thoroughly and decide if changes need to be made. It was silent as they studied their documents. There were some slight changes that were easily corrected. Their last show would be the last Saturday in December. Herb called for a show of hands to verify, and was so noted by Herb's secretary, who was present.

"These documents show The Kentuckians will be dissolved on Saturday, December 30th as will be noted in your own document. As you have no questions concerning your retirement document, we can close the meeting. Agreed?" Silence. "Your final documents will be ready next Thursday for you to sign. Gentlemen, it has been a pleasure to be your attorney for all these years. I wish you happiness in your new endeavors."

"Yes, Herb, you have been a great help," Grant acknowledged. They agreed and slowly walked out of the office.

"Boys, I think we need to stop for a drink! Are you game?" Grant invited.

"Yes!" they chimed in.

"Follow me!"

They ended up at their favorite bar across from the old Grand Old Opry.

It was happy hour and crowded. They knew everybody. Shouts and greetings filled the bar. Word was out about retirement. They pestered them for details. Somebody pushed chairs and tables together to make one long table. Several pints of beer arrived with glasses. Buster, the owner, said "Beer on the house! Just beer, none of the hard stuff. You will run me out of business!" They roared with laughter as they moved to the table. The Kentuckians were mute about their plans, but after a while, it didn't matter. Beer kept flowing. The phone started ringing with their other halves wanting them to come home. It cleared out fast, including the band. The guys were in a huggy mood, even though they would see each other the next day. After hugs were shared around, they slowly drove away.

Grant was feeling quite good when he carefully went up the steps of his house. Tillie was expecting him and helped him through the door.

"My, my, Mr. Grant, you sure look like you had a fine time retiring!" She scolded. He giggled and wandered off to bed with Jake leading the way.

An hour later, the phone rang. "What the?" Grant rolled over and promptly fell off the bed, landing on Jake, who yelped. "Where is the damned thing," he moaned. "Oh, yah," he muttered.

"Hello?" He grumbled.

"Grant, this is Gus at the GOP. We know your last day is Saturday December 30th. We want you to close the show that night." He laughed. He thought Grant sounded like he was already celebrating his retirement.

"Who? What did you say? Close the show?"

"Yes, Grant. What do you say? You need a while to let me know?" He grinned.

"Huh uh, I will." He hung up and went to sleep on the floor.

This time, Gus laughed out loud and marked down a 'yes.' He began to plan the rest of the show for that night.

Grant slept there all night. When he woke up, he shook his head. 'I think I am closing the show on our last night. How do I know this?

Oh, God, I remember now!' He quickly called Gus, apologized, and said of course they will do it. Gus told him he had said OK and was now working on the show. They would be getting in touch with him soon.

He told the guys when he met them at the bus barn that night. What a great finish!

The next Thursday they drove separately to Herb's office. He planned to discuss each document with each recipient. Grant was last. The original paperwork was correct, and they will leave it as such for now.

"I am sure if Bella and I get married, I will need to change my will. But I also want to spend some of my savings on something important to me. Bella's father and mother-in law are selling their portion of the ranch, which is 25%. Her son, Jeremy, wants to sell his 12/1/2 %. I want to buy them. I have not discussed it with Bella yet, but plan to while I am there for Thanksgiving. I plan to make my home in Montana. So, what do we do?"

"I can start working on this now. I will probably work with their attorneys. I am so very happy for you, Grant! No one deserves this more than you! We will continue working together for a while."

"Thank you, Herb, and I will get back with you as soon as I have something permanent."

Grant left Herb's office with a smile on his face and anxious to see Bella. He called her when he got home but did not give her the details about his will or buying percentage of the ranch.

The few weeks left before Thanksgiving sped by. He was on the plane to Montana for the Thanksgiving holidays. Bella was standing where he left her, waiting for him by the gate. She met him and he swirled her around and kissed her.

"How's my girl?" he asked, breathlessly.

"Dying for you to get here!"

"I am, and we have a lot of things to discuss this time."

"Oh, it's yes, yes, yes to whatever you want!"

"I hope so, Bella, honey. It's changes, for sure.!"

Everyone on the ranch was too busy for intimate discussions. Bella didn't pressure him for details. Wednesday night Jeremy and Lillian arrived from Washington, D.C. They were staying until Friday morning, then leaving for the East Coast, spending Thanksgiving with her family. Grant was impressed with this straightforward and courteous young man and his attractive and intelligent wife. They seemed to accept him. Both spent time visiting with him and were interested in his career, especially his songwriting, which was a surprise to Grant. Most people cared less about his writing; they wanted to hear about his stage career.

The same group would be here for dinner, except Greg and Tiffany. She was adamant about going to her family's Thanksgiving. Grant was happy about that. Tom thought Greg was still grieving over Whit. Bella did notice it was the first year without Sam, Edna and Whit. She did not let it spoil this new blessed event. Meg and Clark, Nancy and Tom and their kids, Jesse and Amy, and Jeremy and Lillian. Tammy asked Bella if she and Grant could come for Sunday dinner after church. She was trying hard to get on Grant's good side. Bella said they would not be to church. Things like that were not feasible yet. She promised to ask him, hoping he would say yes. Tammy was her best friend, even though she makes lots of faux paus.

Jesse and Jeremy spent most of Thanksgiving Eve night catching up on each other's lives. Jesse did most of the talking as Jeremy's work was classified.

"I did one thing since Dad died. He never wanted to have the ranch surveyed for oil. I have hired a well-known oil drilling company from Taos, New Mexico to come and look. They are the southwest district for Carson Oil Well Drilling Company based in New Jersey. They have an extremely high rating and fair pricing. I called the CEO, Cal Lawson, a few weeks ago. We had a good visit. His geologist and crew will be coming soon. His brother, Varen, the company pilot and general manager, will bring the crew and equipment. Wouldn't that be a hoot if we have oil?"

"Don't get your hopes up too much, Jesse. Dad didn't think there was any oil."

"Well, if there is, Cal promised me they will start drilling in the spring." He would not let Jeremy discourage him.

Thanksgiving Day was chaotic, but fun. They used the large kitchen table and benches. The table was able to hold the 25-pound turkey and trimmings. The meal got underway at 2:30 p.m. Maria and her crew did a fabulous job serving, and putting up with the women who each had their own opinion on how to do everything, from basting the turkey to whipping cream for the pies.

Nancy put Fiona, their 18-month-old daughter, in a highchair close to her at the end of the table. Tom did the best he could to make Thomas, 5 ½, sit on a "big boy" chair next to him. Nancy put mashed potatoes and peas on a small dish for Fiona, who promptly threw it onto the table. She started screaming. Nancy and Bella ran for towels to wipe up what they could. Nancy tried again with no peas. Things quieted for a while. Eating and visiting continued until Thomas rubbed cranberry sauce over his face. He wanted to get out of his chair. Tom wiped as much of the cranberry sauce off Thomas's face and put him down. He ran around the table, yelling at the top of his voice. Nancy grabbed him as he came around her corner. He had a tantrum and threw himself on the floor. Fiona loved this and banged her spoon on the highchair. Nancy burst into tears. Tom got up.

"Nancy, stop crying and get their coats. I'll hold them and help you get them on. Bella, thank you for this lovely dinner. I do apologize." They tried to get the kids' coats on, but with no luck. They quickly exited the party. There was complete silence. Then, one by one, each person started to laugh until they all were. They finished their dinner in peace. Jesse, Amy, Jeremy, and Lillian were thankful they had no children.

Meg and Clark left at 6 p.m. The young people left for drinks in town. Bella and Grant sat on the couch and looked at each other. They burst out laughing hysterically.

"Come on, Bella, honey, let's go upstairs, drink wine and soak in the hot tub," he suggested after they caught their breaths.

"I'll get the wine and the glasses. You start the tub!"

They were relieved their first Thanksgiving Dinner was over.

Chapter 17

They had one week to plan the rest of their lives. Friday morning was quiet. Bella and Grant were enjoying morning coffee. Jesse took Jeremy and Lillian to the airport in Missoula. Amy had meetings with clients.

"Let's go into my office. I need to check emails and any other problem that arose over Thanksgiving."

"You sure you want me to stay?"

"Yes. You can learn some of the things I deal with."

They took their coffee into the office. She pulled up her emails and chose which ones were important. Grant watched her quietly until she leaned back and took a sip of coffee.

"When are we going to get married?" he asked bluntly.

"This week is fine," she offered as she shut down the computer. May as well start on Friday morning.

"Bella, can we wait until after the last show? I want to get married here without rushing and not all that news coverage that we would have in Nashville."

"So, you are serious! OK, sometime after New Year's and you are moved up here. I love the way we get things done! What are you bringing?"

"I am going to list the house when I get back. I wanted to be sure we were getting married. I need to go through my things, and I'd like you to see if there is anything you want. Other than that, I might do something stupid and sell it furnished. It's funny how I don't care about anything now that I have you. After we get married, we can decide where we are going to live. If you want to stay here, that's fine. You can fix it up any way you want or leave it as is."

"I am so happy you aren't rushing me. Yes, these are decisions we need to make quietly.

"I want to come to the show. That way I can see everything. Oh, this is so exciting! How can I wait another day!"

"Honey, we have waited all these years, we can wat a few more weeks! I will be busy getting our final show together, going through things, and selling the house. Right now, I feel we have taken care of a few big things. I may as well go on with the biggest, outside of finalizing our wedding." He shut the door.

"Bella, I want to buy Sam's 25% and Jerey's 12 1/2 % of the ranch, if you all approve. I have talked to my lawyer in Nashville. He is working on the paperwork and will be waiting for you and your family's OK. This is a big deal for all of us, Bella. Everything must be agreed upon. This will be my home and my life, and yours, too. What do you think?" He took a deep sigh, looking at her.

She got up from her chair and walked to him. He stood up and they embraced. He took her face in his hands as they gazed into each other's eyes. He closed his eyes and kissed her softly. She wrapped her arms around him and put her lips on his neck. He felt tears, but wasn't sure if it was just her's, or his.

"Let's go for a walk. We can get jackets from the mud room. I can't think of anything more appropriate right now."

They strolled past the buildings and out to the corral. Blue and Queen were there and came over to nuzzle them. They caressed the horses' velvet noses, and they nickered softly. Grant felt like they were welcoming him. They walked on towards the pasture and watched the cattle. The cattle drive had happened, and they were here for the winter. A few cows saw them and wandered over to them, curious. They stretched their necks out and snorted to pick up Bella's and Grant's scents. They stood, arm in arm, looking at them, noticing their soft, furry winter coats. The cows' curiosity was satisfied and moved away. They, too, moved away and went back to the house.

Maria served them hot home-made chicken noodle soup and warm bread with soft butter. They drank hot tea with pieces of lemon cake. Arms entwined; they went upstairs. No words were spoken. None were needed. They still had plenty of days to make more plans.

Saturday morning, it was Bella's turn to ask questions. They took their coffee into the office. This place became the decision-making room.

"Tammy has invited us to Sunday dinner tomorrow after church. I told her we would not be going to church right now. She so wants you to like her! I am sure you will like Jeff; he is considerate and a good mediator due to his line of work. We could go about 12:30. Please say yes, Grant," she pleaded. He didn't answer right away. Several thoughts went through his mind.

"Where do they live? Is it close to the freeway? Is there a police and fire department? Anybody else be there?" She was surprised at the inquiries.

"Bella, you have no idea how careful entertainers must be. Even I have had terrible, and some disgusting, things happen to me. I felt safe here, and in town, but when you get to people's homes, you never know what could be waiting. Even if it's not their doing."

"No, I've never thought of any of that. They are a couple of miles from the freeway. They are in a cul-de-sac. Yes, we have paid police and fire departments. Not volunteers. No one will be there but us and Terry, their teenage son. Will that help?" She hoped this would reassure him. He did not mention what a teenager could do.

"OK, let's give it a try. I will be busy being nice to Tammy and watching my back!" He joked.

"Thanks, my love! I'll call her now."

Tammy was relieved, but nervous, hoping she could make him comfortable. Jeff said, "Don't worry, we'll have fun."

That settled, she moved on to the next problem. "OK, I need to call Sam and Eda. That will be difficult. Jeremy next. Can you excuse me for a while?"

"Fine. I'll go up to the bedroom and do my own calling."

She said a little prayer as she dialed Sam. He recognized her number."

"What do you want?" He bellowed. It was strange to hear this man who had been an important person during her marriage.

"Good morning, Sam. I have good news for you and Edna."

"Spit it out," he grumbled.

"I have a buyer for your share of the ranch," she began. He interrupted her.

"So, when do we get the money?"

"Within a week or so."

"That long? I want it sooner. Who bought it?"

"You know I don't have to tell you, per your contract."

"Aha! It's that country singer Gene Autrey wanna-be, isn't it?" How did he know, she wondered.

"Yes, it's Grant Bartlett. He is paying cash," She made her voice civil and non-competitive.

"So, you are shacking up with him! Edna, did you hear this? That son of a bitch she has been having an affair with all these years is buying our son's ranch!" How did he know that, too? She felt nauseous.

"Sam, I am going to hang up now. I wanted you to know your portion was purchased." She hung up the phone gently and clasped her hands together. She wondered if he had some form of dementia, this strong, capable cattle baron roaring like a madman. She felt sorry for both. Poor Edna!

She was looking forward to calling Jeremy. She was sure she would get a better response. She dialed his cell phone.

"Jeremy! So glad you answered!' she exclaimed joyously.

"Mom! Hi! Are you OK?"

"Yes! I have some great news for you! Grant bought your portion of the ranch! He also bought Sam's. That did not go well. I hope your response will be better."

"That's just great! He wants to be a part of you and your life! Does Jesse know?"

"I haven't told him yet. I'm not sure how he will react. Grant has no interest in running the ranch. You are right, he just wants to be here with me. Thank you, sweetheart! You have made my day!"

"OK. We are trying to get time off to come to the show. I applied for a week. We plan on a nice trip driving. Wish us luck! Bye!"

She wasn't looking forward to explaining it to Jesse. She planned on talking to him when he came into the house for coffee. She didn't have long to wait. He came bursting into her office carrying a mug of coffee and four donuts. "I came in for coffee!" He gobbled most of the donuts, getting crumbs on his mouth and shirt.

"OK but sit down for a minute. I have something to tell you."

"Oh oh! That doesn't sound good!'

"No, it's not bad. But Grant bought Sam's and Jeremy's portions of the ranch! He wants to stay here with me. He has no interest in being involved with the running of the ranch. He just wants to retire and be here with me. Jesse, I want you to understand this. He is no threat to you or the ranch. Please tell me you see that."

"Well, I don't know what to think. He will have 37 ½% of the ranch, more than me.

"But this is your ranch, and it will be when I am gone. I will talk to Todd to see if we need some legal documents, more than my will. We can easily make some kind of document that says Grant will not interfere. Please, Jesse. I just went through hell with Sam! "

"Well, we will just have to wait and see," he said dejectedly. He stood up and spilled coffee on her desk and the front of his shirt. Spurs jingling, he walked out. 'He is so like his dad, walking just like him.' She noticed he had his gun belt on, even his dad's chaps. She hadn't thought to ask him where he was going. She loved him and hated to see him upset.

Sunday morning found Tammy unable to get one word of the sermon. She kept wringing her hands together until Jeff took them in his. She was terrified wondering what she might do to set Grant off. By the time they got home she was in tears, knowing her dinner would be a flop. Jeff did all he could in the kitchen to help and Terry set the table. She had a small glass of wine before frying the chicken. Jeff mashed the potatoes with lots of cream and butter.

Grant and Bella arrived at 12:30. The fragrance of fried chicken came from the kitchen. Tammy greeted them with flushed and flour-coated cheeks.

"Come in! Welcome!" She ushered them into their lovely home as Jeff came to greet them. "Welcome to our humble home!" he offered. It was not humble. Art décor covered the soft grey walls. Elegant blue living room furniture was placed attractively and led eyes into the dining room. Tammy had Terry set the table with old white china trimmed in gold. Gold silverware encircled the plates. White cloth napkins were folded so they stood up on the plates.

Jeff took them into the warm kitchen as Tammy continued frying the chicken.

"Sit down at our small booth here and have a glass of wine while the chicken fryer finishes her duties!" They watched her skillfully transfer golden pieces of chicken onto a huge platter that matched the dinner plates. Jeff carried it into the dining room. Bella helped carry bowls of steaming potatoes, gravy and vegetables. Bread was already on the table. Iced water was in heavy crystal goblets.

Jeff called Terry to the table. Tammy tried hard to quit sweating. "Terry, this is Grant Bartlett, Bella's good friend. Of course, you already know Bella. Grant, this is our son, Terry."

"Glad to meet you, Terry!" Grant stood up to shake his hand.

"Gosh, Mr. Bartlett, I love your music! I have several of your albums. Mom told me how they went to see you in Missoula a long time ago." The young man was straight-forward and personable. Grant thought they should be proud of him.

They sat around the table. Tammy drank all her water. Jeff refilled it for her. Jeff had a short prayer of thanksgiving and began passing food.

Conversation was light while they were eating but became lively and fun. Everyone entered the conversation, even Terry. They helped clean the table, then Jeff asked if Grant would like to play poker. Grant was surprised, but said sure, he loved five-card draw. The guys went to the game room and Terry went to his room, hoping to talk with Grant again some time. Bella and Tammy cleaned the kitchen. Bella tried to reassure Tammy that things were going great. They went to the game room and played along with the guys. Betting got wild and poker chips changed hands frequently.

At 4 o-clock they went to the dining room for chocolate cake and coffee. They were looking forward to getting together after Grant arrived permanently.

Tammy was exhausted. She did feel much happier about the Grant situation. Jeff held Tammy in his arms for a long time after they left. "Tammy, you were wonderful! The meal was perfect, and they loved it! I think everything is fine now between you and Grant. I love you to the moon and back, I don't care if that is an old expression. You are my darling!" Tammy cried tears of happiness and thanksgiving.

Grant and Bella were enjoying the hot tub with glasses of wine. The day was pure joy for them, to have new friends when Grant arrived permanently. Grant continued to sing praises about Terry. "Bella, honey, I have accepted Tammy as she is and there should be no hard feelings between us. Jeff will be a good friend to me and will help me be included in the town." These words warmed her heart. Later they were in bed, remembering they had only 3 days left before
Grant flew back to Nashville on Thursday.

The next three days were spent quietly at the ranch. They took long walks around the compound. Once they walked to the pasture where the work horses were kept. As they stood against the fence, one horse lifted her head and neighed and galloped at Bella. She slid to a stop and put her head over the fence. Bella scratched the blaze on her forehead.

"Hello, Sweetheart! How are you?" she cooed. The horse lifted her head and nickered.

"OK, what have we here?" Grant questioned.

"This is Anita. She is my horse. Whit bought her for me several years ago. She too, had been spayed, like Queen. Whit broke her, or I should say 'horse whispered' her, if there is such a word. He had that special way about him." 'Oh, I should not have said that' she thought. Grant stared at the ground.

"She is a beauty! How come you named her Anita?" She had a deep brown coat, almost black, and the blaze on her face was white. Four white hooves pranced for Bella.

"I don't know why; it just is Anita."

Grant tried hard to spend time with Jesse, but most of the time Jesse revoked his attention and moved away. Grant decided he would have to wait until he was here permanently, and Jesse would see he was no threat.

Grant learned what ranch life was like in these three days. He was fascinated how the machinery delivered hay to the cows into long rows of mangers. They also got pellets of extra nutrients. There were square blocks of salt distributed throughout the pasture. He watched the cowboys riding out to check the pasture fence and other things. Bella tried to explain the workings as best she could. Grant decided he would get acquainted with the cowboys when he got back. She took him to the large dining room where someone was always eating huge meals. He loved it all.

Thursday morning, they said goodbye for the last time. She stood by the gate and waved as he left. She would be joining him in Nashville the day after Christmas. They thought they could stand being apart for that long.

Chapter 18

Buzzy met him at the airport. He warned the city and airport police Grant was arriving. He didn't think there would be a problem as Grant was dressed in old jeans and a baseball cap pulled low, but still, he wanted safety for his friend. Grant arrived and hurried to meet Buzzy, quickly exited the airport, and got into Buzzy's car.

"How are you doing? Everything still on schedule?" Buzzy was concerned.

"Yes, it's great! It was worth waiting for. But I've got lots of things to do before I can leave. Come in when we get home. I need to talk to you."

There were a few onlookers when they arrived at the house. Police stood cautiously around them. "Hay, why are you quitting? Getting too old? Hahaha!" Tillie had the door open, and they ran in. "OK, the show's over! Get going!" the police suggested without raising their voices or brandishing a gun or stick. They groaned and made rude comments, then drifted away.

"Oh Mr. Grant! Glad you are home! Anxious to hear everything!" Tillie was always relieved when he returned from any of his adventures.

Jake was happy too. He ran to Grant. Grant swooped him up and put him on his shoulder. Buzzy wondered what he was going to do about Jake.

"Tillie, we are going to talk later. Buzzy, sit down." Tillie and Jake left.

"Here's my biggest worry right now. I'm going to list my house. I am…"

"No! Don't list your house!"

"Why not?"

"I'll buy it!"

"What?"

"I'll buy it! Mary Lou loves it! She says if he ever wants to sell it, we'll buy it! Every time we have been here, she says it. So, I'll buy it!"

"Well, OK, but what I was trying to say is, I want to sell it furnished. We plan to start over and I'm not taking anything with me."

"That's fine. If there is something we don't like, we will sell it, or something. We need new furniture anyway, and yours is hardly used. Our stuff is shot, with four kids and now grandkids, it's pretty beat up. So, what do you want for it?"

"Geez, Buzzy, I have no idea! Let Herb figure it out. There is a real estate attorney in his office, we'll use him. Sound good?"

"Great! Anything else to discuss? If not, I'm going home to tell Mary Lou we are moving!" He did a little dance as he left.

'Well, I'll be damned! I'm going to call Bella right now.'

Monday morning, he called Herb and told him about Buzzy buying the house.

"How fortunate! Let me transfer you to Raymond Betts, our real estate lawyer."

Raymond set an appointment for Grant, Buzzy and Mary Lou to come into his office to finalize the deal. This went well. Buzzy would take position the day Grant moved out. Grant ordered packing boxes from the moving company he hired and began packing things he wanted to take. By the time Bella arrived, there were just a few more things to go through, then the moving company would haul them to Montana.

Wednesday was the day he had the talk with Tillie. He was not looking forward to it. She sat him down with a huge piece of chocolate cream pie and fresh coffee.

"You aren't making this any easier."

"Mr. Grant, let me do it for you, just like I did when you hired me. Of course, you must let me go. I will be fine! I know you will leave me a great severance package; you don't even have to tell me what it is. I might not go to work right away. Might visit kids and grandkids. I can get a job with any of you guys. I will be choosy; you have made me that way. So, the only thing left to settle is, how much longer, and what are you going to do with Jake? You cannot ship him to Montana and to a new home. I will take him, if you want."

Grant had stopped eating to stare at Tillie. Yes, she covered everything.

"Tillie, I love you, you know that. Wish I could take you and Jake with me, and I can do neither. I'm not sure of the exact date for you to leave and let me think about Jake." He finished his pie. Tillie poured more coffee for them.

"That's OK, you just tell me when and if." They finished their coffee. He went back to his packing, and she went downstairs to her room.

Christmas was forgotten this year. There wasn't time to celebrate. They promised each other the holiday next year would be fantastic. Bella arrived the day after, as promised. Buzzy contacted the city police and airport security just in case. He drove Grant to the airport, then went into the terminal to pick her up. They knew each other instantly. Grant said to watch for a nervous skinny guy with thick horn-rimmed glasses, probably pacing, and that would be Buzzy. Grant said Bella would be the prettiest woman leaving the plane. Buzzy decided that was Grant's description. Bella ran to Buzzy. When he saw her, he agreed she was one of the prettiest. He was partial to his own sweet Mary Lou.

"I'm so happy to meet you!" They said at the same time. They laughed and waited at the carousel for her luggage. A few paparazzi recognized Buzzy and asked him who this woman was. Buzzy didn't say. They snapped their picture, and it appeared in the scandal papers that Buzzy was having an affair. Grant was furious, as was Mary Lou. They decided to ignore it; that would make it blow over faster. Later, it was fun when they realized it was Grant's girlfriend. The editor published an apology.

Buzzy retrieved her luggage and they hurried to Buzzy's dark-windowed SUV. The paparazzi followed but did not see Grant in the back. They were ecstatic to see each other, but sat apart, visiting. Buzzy pulled into Grant's driveway with paparazzi behind the car. Police shooed them away. After they were safely gone, Buzzy led Bella and Grant through the open door past Tillie.

"Here you are, safe and sound! Now, enjoy! See you Saturday night, if not sooner," he threw at them.

"Welcome, Miss Bella! Been waiting a long time to meet you! "

"I feel like I know you, Tillie!" The women shared a quick hug.

Grant and Jake led Bella to his bedroom. He tossed her luggage to the floor and did what they were longing for. She was in his arms and on the bed. Jake interrupted them. They laughed and pushed him off the bed. He ended the magic for now. They went to the kitchen for the lunch Tillie had left. He showed her the house and she loved it. "Another time and another place and I could have lived here," she told him. The next few days they worked on what to take to Montana. He kept insisting he only wanted his personal things, including all his music and guitars. She stood in his closet door caressing the sleeve of his blue velvet suit.

"What are you going to do with all your fancy suits?"

"There is a small museum located by the old Ryman auditorium that shows outfits from entertainers from years ago, like the 30's. They are coming for them. I am saving one, the one you are touching, and will wear it Saturday night. It is the one I wore the first time I saw you."

"Yes, it is! So, we will keep it forever!" She remembered how she wanted to touch his sleeve that night.

"And my boots with the rhinestone toes, and one hat, the one I will use Saturday. Yes, some things are too special to part with." He looked away, remembering.

The museum curator arrived the next day. He was pleased to have Grant's suits, even the new, more casual ones. He wasn't sure how he was going to display them but told him he would let him know and send pictures. Grant put on a brave front, but he was sad and emotional as they were rolled out to the van on a mobile hanger used in resorts. He walked away. Bella did not follow him; he needed the time alone.

Friday night Jeremy and Lillian arrived. They enjoyed their road trip and planned to go on a different road back to D.C. They checked into a hotel the couples had made reservations for earlier in the week. Jesse and Amy flew in on Saturday morning and would fly home Sunday morning as he didn't want to be away from the ranch very long. Bella and Grant met them at noon for lunch. Grant needed to be behind the scenes. The lunch went well, but they could see Grant was preoccupied. Their mother was beaming. Jeremy was happy for her, but Jesse had doubts. The girls thought the situation would be fine and tried to reassure Jesse. Grant had to leave before lunch was over. Jeremy and the wives gave Grant big hugs, while Jesse would only shake his hand. Bella looked at Jesse like she did when he was a boy, saying 'you are not behaving nicely,' which he ignored. Bella held Grant close. "You look so handsome! And you are mine! I love you so much!" He kissed her quickly and went backstage. The family sat down in their front row center seats to watch the complete show. They were in awe as each famous entertainer came on stage. They had never thought about seeing them in person. The last performer bowed and left the stage in a flurry of curtains swinging shut. The lights were dimmed.

Suddenly, Grant's theme song began. The curtains were drawn back slowly. The lights were quickly turned up. Grant's theme played louder and faster. Grant came out of the wings waving his hat furiously as he walked up and down the stage. The crowd was in a frenzy, stomping, screaming, clapping. Grant hung his hat on the back of a stool, grabbed his guitar and walked to the microphone. He strummed the chord he always used, and the crowd quieted. They knew what he was going to say: "Are you ready for some good country music?" They went wild again. The final show of Grant Bartlett and the Kentuckians was beginning!

They played the old songs and a few newer ones. He sat on the stool and put his hat back on and told the crowd Rick was going to take over. "Now, Rick here is going to take over for a while. I can't play lead guitar, so I'll just chord a little bit. That OK with you?" They continued their noise and accepted Rick's versions of the songs. Grant took center stage again. Shortly, Buzzy came on stage. He took the mic away from Grant and said: "We have a little surprise for you, Grant, and the guys! How about we get started with Garth. Garth, come on out!" Suddenly, the stage was filled with every country music singer in the country. Each one of the most famous had a short message for Grant and wished him well as he starts a new chapter in his life.

Bella was taken from her seat to stand with Grant. He told the crowd this was the new joy in his life. The crowd clapped, then

Buzzy came back. "Come on, Grant. I have the limo waiting for you and Bella at the stage entrance. Say a quick goodbye," he whispered. Grant looked at him gratefully. "Well guess this is it everybody! Bella and I want to thank you from the bottom of our hearts!" He signaled for the band to start his theme song. He held on to Bella and waved his hat as he exited the stage, Buzzy close at hand. The crowd on the stage made an opening for them, but still stopped him for one last handshake or hug.

Buzzy led them through the throng until they got to the stage door. He held it open and led them to the waiting limo. He practically shoved them in and shut the door. The limo driver sped away. They sat staring at each other. Grant had tears running down his cheeks. Bella found a cloth napkin for him. After he quieted down, she opened a bottle of water, which he drank quickly. "Thanks," he croaked, then laid his head on her shoulder. They rode that way home. Buzzy beat them there, making sure a few policemen were there to control the crowd. Strangely, there were few people there. He was relieved.

They walked into the bedroom. Bella helped him get his sweat-soaked suit off. She tossed it on the floor, just like he used to do. He laid on the outside covers of the bed and fell asleep instantly. She took her things off and laid down beside him. They never moved until morning.

They used Sunday to recuperate. The kids left without seeing them, which was fine. By evening, they were ready for food. Grant ordered pizzas and salads with a bottle of wine. By Tuesday, they were ready to face the world.

Tuesday morning, Grant called the moving company who promised to arrive by 5 p.m. Grant and Bella went through every room again, looking in corners of closets and drawers. Everything seemed to be in order. They packed the clothes, etc., they would need for the long drive to Montana. They left a spot for Jake's things in case they had to take him. Grant hadn't decided on Jake's future yet.

Tillie was doing some cleaning. She wanted to wait until they were gone before she did the heavy stuff. Grant called her to their usual spot at the kitchen table for their final discussion. Since he was leaving dishes, pots and pans and coffee pot, she made the last pot for him. The pies were gone. They sat looking at each other as they knew this was the end.

"Tillie, I think we well discussed everything. Come in after we leave. Lock up and leave the keys in the garage for Buzzy. I have a check for you right here. I could never say what you mean to me. I'm still not sure about Jake. What would you do with him when you go to visit your kids and grandkids?"

"I would take him with me because they are close. I have been happy here, Mr. Grant. But I know you must get on with your life. I know I would love Bella and could take care of her too, if she were staying here. Leaving you is the hardest one for me. But like I told you, some guy will need me, just like you did. And don't worry about me, just like I won't worry about you!" They laughed at the last statement. She left them and would be back after they were gone the next day.

The moving company arrived at 3 p.m. Grant's boxes were loaded by 4. Barney, the driver, said he would take 3 days to get to Montana.

"Things will be fine, Mr. Bartlett. Here is my cell phone number and the bill of lading. You can contact me any time. You know I've hauled you entertainers all over the US. Since you are taking it easy going back, I'm sure I'll be there before you. Miss Bella, you still want me to call this number, Jesse's cell phone, when I get there?"

"Yes, please. There will be plenty of cowboys to help you unload. Thanks for everything!" Barney waved as he pulled into the street.

"Tomorrow, we leave, Bella, honey! I need to wait for Buzzy. I'm sure he will be here early. I had the guy at the car dealership fill the gas tank, so we should be fine for the day. I am going to love being out on the road, not stuffed into the bus! Just like an ordinary guy, which I am!"

"Remember, we are going to stop and look at something interesting if we want to. I am so excited! Not a care in the world!"

They ordered Chinese for dinner and laughed at their fortune cookies. Buzzy woke them up at 7 a.m. the next day. He and Grant ironed out a few problems. They were walking down the hall when Jake ran in front of them and went under Grant's bed.

"We may as well catch him now and get him in his carrier," Grant fretted.

Buzzy retrieved him and handed him to Grant. He jumped out of Grant's arms and got in the middle of the bed and began grooming himself. Buzzy reached for him again. Jake clung to him and wouldn't let Grant take him. He began purring.

"Now what?" Grant was getting exasperated.

"Grant, I'll take him. He belongs here. This is his home. He will be happy here and Mary Lou will love him and take good care of him. She won't let the grandkids pester him. OK?"

"Well, I guess. He's been a part of me for so many years. Geez, Buzzy, I guess you can keep him. Let's get his stuff out of the trunk."

"What's going on?" Bella followed them to the car as they unloaded Jake's things.

"He wouldn't come to me! He plopped himself on the bed and stayed. Breaks my heart, but I am leaving him here."

"Oh, Grant! Are you sure? It was fine with me to take him home!"

"I know, but just think of all the work. He will be fine with Buzzy."

Grant didn't go back into the house to say goodbye to Jake. He never came out of the bedroom. Grant was in tears, and he felt silly. Bella patted his leg. They waved goodbye to Buzzy and left Nashville for Montana. Buzzy turned to go back in the house. He saw Jake sitting in the picture window staring at the departing car.

They stayed a few days in Las Vegas. Grant rented a room from the hotel where he played so many concerts. It was fun to be 'on the other side' for a change. They gambled and tried to see a show, but too many people recognized him. One night they were driving by a wedding chapel. Grant turned around and parked in the parking lot.

"Let's get married!" he said, excited.

"OK let's! Now!"

They rushed in like naughty teenagers running away to get married.

"We want to get married now!" insisted Grant.

"That would be just dandy, Mr. Bartlett!" Elvis agreed.

Elvis did the paperwork, started the wedding march. Priscilla was matron of honor.

They stood by a beat-up trellis with dusty fake flowers as Elvis read the wedding vows, then he burst into one of his popular love songs. Grant gave him $500.00. They weren't sure if they were legally married, but tonight it didn't matter. They would check it out when they got home. Later they will have a reception for everyone. They felt like they were those teenagers as they went to their hotel room.

The next day they turned north for Montana. Bella's cell phone rang. It was Jesse.

"Hi, son!"

"Mom!"

"Yes. Jesse?"

"We have oil! Cal Lawson said the drilling crew will be coming to drill in the spring!"